NOW YOU
SEE IT

NOW YOU SEE IT

A NOVEL

CORNELIA NIXON

HarperPerennial
A Division of HarperCollins*Publishers*

The stories in this collection have appeared in the following magazines and won the following prizes: (1) "Alf's Garage," *Chicago Tribune*, September 11, 1988; The Nelson Algren Awards for Short Fiction, runner-up. (2) "Affection," *Ploughshares*, Spring 1989. (3) "Death Angel," *Black Warrior Review*, Spring 1989; *Black Warrior Review* Award for Fiction, 1988–89. (4) "Now You See It," *Quarterly West* 27, Summer/Fall 1988. (5) "Assumed Identity," *Black Warrior Review*, Winter/Spring 1991.

A hardcover edition of this book was published in 1991 by Little, Brown & Co. It is here reprinted by arrangement with Little, Brown & Co.

HarperCollins books may be purchased for educational, business, or sales promotional use. For information, please call or write: Special Markets Department, HarperCollins Publishers, Inc., 10 East 53rd Street, New York, NY 10022. Telephone: (212) 207-7528; Fax: (212) 207-7222.

First HarperPerennial edition published 1992.

LIBRARY OF CONGRESS CATALOG CARD NUMBER 91-57920

ISBN 0-06-097472-9

92 93 94 95 96 RRD 10 9 8 7 6 5 4 3 2 1

CONTENTS

For Dean
and in memory of H. E. Nixon

❖❖❖

*I would like to thank the Mary
Ingraham Bunting Institute at Radcliffe,
where the first of these stories
were written.*

NOW YOU
SEE IT

ALF'S
GARAGE

❖◈❖

─────────── IN THE SUMMER OF
1949, in eastern Colorado, far from the nearest metric
wrench, our car died and sank into a sea of sheep. At
first we did not realize what was coming. It appeared
to be a low yellow fog on the road ahead, strange
enough in such a waterless place. Driving closer, we
saw thin-legged, black-faced bodies fat with quivering wool, rushing and leaping in a wild flood kept
whole by black silky-haired dogs trotting along
beside it, waving their plumey tails. Driving up to
the edge, we went into a roar of sheep bleats, dog
yelps and thousands of shuffling hooves. Dust and a
hot meaty stink rolled through the car.

"Stop! What are you doing? Not so close!" my
wife yelled over the noise, holding on to Hank, our
youngest, who was dancing on her lap with his hard
white shoes. In the back seat, David, age three, and

3

Charlie, four, were on their feet crowing with excitement.

I stopped when the fender brushed wool. The engine gave a final run of high fast hammering, two low coughs, and died. I took hold of Hank and climbed out, sheep brushing my knees. I let David and Charlie squeeze out onto the running board and hold on to the top of the door, while I braced it open with my body. Sheep surged around the car as if it were a boulder, dogs rushing wide to turn them back on the other side.

Too late I noticed that they were not moving past but toward us. In a moment we were so deep in, no dirt was visible in any direction. Sheep scrambled onto the hood of the car with their cloven hooves, launched themselves off it into the bobbing mass. One big ram tried to go over the top, slipped on the windshield and sprawled on the roof inches from Charlie's head before he turned and flung himself off.

Hank dug his tiny fingernails into my neck, keening a high thin note. David solemnly tracked individual sheep with his eyes, jerking one hand forward, trying to touch them. I glanced grinning at Charlie, and he was howling in terror, tears pouring out of wide white eyes.

I gripped his shoulder and shouted. "Hey, don't worry, buddy! It's all right! They're only sheep!" He was beyond hearing, sucking his breath in deep jabs, shooting horrified glances this way and that, a world overrun with sheep.

Gradually, under the uproar I heard another sound, made by my wife, who knelt on the driver's seat with both arms around David and Charlie, shrieking words I knew I'd have plenty of time to make out when the sheep were gone. On the horizon, sheepboys crept closer on dark horses. When they arrived, wearing chaps and wide hats, they grinned at us with white teeth, turning their horses' necks with loose reins.

The tide receded from around the car. We were parked at an angle, half on the road, half on the shoulder, in a welter of hoofprints, tufts of wool and bits of trampled dung. Charlie sniffed and hiccupped, but as soon as I let go of the door he jumped down and ran after the sheep. David trailed behind him, and Hank squirmed to get down. I held on to him, though there wasn't another car in sight.

Ella untangled her legs from the steering wheel and climbed out. I was surprised to see that she was crying. The few times she'd done it — when I got on a ship to go to war and when I came back and when Charlie was born — she seemed ashamed, and didn't make much of it. She wasn't crying much now in the way of tears, but her face was trembling out of shape and her eyes looked ready to jump out of it and pummel me.

"It was not enough that you *forced* us to get into this *time bomb* with you — no, you had to go *looking* for some way to get us *trampled* to *death* —"

"Sheep-trampling being the number three cause of death in the western United States, right after lizard-tripping and —"

"I suppose it gave you a sort of *thrill* — you are about as responsible as a — as a — *mocking thrush* —"

"Mockingbird," I said.

Hank was resting peacefully on my hip, sucking his thumb, but she yanked him away from me and walked up the highway, toward the older boys. Over her shoulder Hank gave me an it's-your-own-damn-fault-buddy look. Like Ella, he had large eyes the color of swimming pools, and accusation was their natural mode.

I stood still and let the Rage of the Married pass through me, keeping all of my limbs relaxed, so they could not begin to smash, rend or crush without my permission. Facing away from the highway, I let the parched wind blow through me, east to west.

◈◈◈

For weeks before we left, Ella had informed me that the car would not make it across the country. She was German, had grown up in Switzerland, and had no respect for machines that did not whir along with the precision of the average cuckoo clock. This one, a

1937 Lancia Aprilia, had probably been a fine car at one time, but now, twelve years old, it sometimes refused to start and the transmission rattled like dice. I knew nothing whatever about it, apart from how to give its name the proper Italian roll. Probably it should have gone to a mechanic before we left, but we were in an awkward period between the end of my allowance under the G.I. Bill and my first paycheck, which we wouldn't see until I made it to Berkeley and taught for a month.

"We'll just have to hope for the best," I said, as we got ready to go.

"You — you think a car runs on goodwill — you think it cares about us! 'Won't let us down,' because we need it! You think the world is made of cream cheese!"

Even when she wasn't asked, she could explain how that had happened to me: I had never had to take care of myself, someone had always done it for me (my mother, Harvard, the navy, my wife). I would've starved without them, since I could lose a ten-dollar bill out of my pocket, leave my key in any door I put it in, and get lost in my own neighborhood. I could not balance the checkbook, fix a leaky faucet or drive a car.

"Hold on," I said. "I'm a perfectly adequate driver." Better than she was, I thought. Pulling out of Cambridge, for instance, we were overloaded —

two adults, three kids and four suitcases strapped on top — but still she had to weave through traffic like a cheetah through a herd of wildebeest. I did not speed and drove well over to the right of the road, leaving an extra margin of safety between us and the other cars.

"Stay in the *middle* of the lane," she said, clutching the armrest on her side. "You are going to hit a tree or a cow or something. People don't *expect* you to be over here."

We took turns watching each other's every move, while behind us the boys each defended a few square feet of sweaty leather upholstery. On the fourth day, I was driving, she was watching, and it was about a hundred degrees in the car, when we reached St. Louis in time for rush-hour traffic. Inching along on shimmering asphalt, I aimed for second and hit reverse. The car gave a murderous clunk and stopped.

"Perhaps you should just get a gun and shoot it," Ella said in her softly burred accent. "Perhaps you should just kill it outright?"

This was in the days before seat belts, and the boys stood up in back, to get a better view of my humiliation.

"You did it, Daddy," Charlie murmured confidentially into my ear.

"The car is fine," I said in a clear voice, over the transmission dice, now rattling distinctly louder.

That night, at a motel in Blue Springs, Missouri, I attempted to encourage the transmission. On previous evenings I had recovered from the day's drive by standing in a swimming pool catching each of the boys eighty or ninety times, but tonight the sky was a menacing green, and the radio promised tornadoes. Ella had the boys bottled up in our room, and the car seemed like a good place to be.

The Lancia had been generously equipped with an English version of the Italian owner's manual, and I went in for some leisurely study by map-reading light. "Attention! Very important! You trouble in hot motoring temperature explicate transmission liquids from among the engine," it advised.

Ah-hah, I thought. Moments later, standing in a deluge of tepid water lit by naked lightning, I explicated that quantity. It was adequate. I turned out the map light and dashed for our room.

The next morning, brilliant waterdrops sparkled on every leaf and blade of grass, but when I pressed the ignition button we heard only a gentle click. Leather creaked as everyone leaned forward to see what would happen next.

It's wonderful, the peaceful sounds a motel makes in the morning: maids banging trolleys through the doorways, shushing dirty sheets into hampers, phawhoomping clean ones open in the air. For a moment I pretended to be a gardener, pausing on his hoe to listen.

"He killed it this time," Charlie explained to the others.

We spent that morning locating a foreign-car mechanic, who replaced the battery I had worn out reading by map light. I bought the boys off with cheeseburgers and chocolate shakes, but Ella was not so easily won. I even let her have the wheel and rode halfway through Kansas with Hank flung stickily across my lap like a pasha on a silk pillow, but she kept her eyes straight ahead, mouth set in a sober line. Grimly she wound the engine to the top of its whine, passed slower cars without wasting a flick of her wrist.

Hour after hour we crested dry swells of wheat, not a house or a cow in sight. Every so often, a tall white silo loomed up on the left, always about a mile from the road.

"Car's running pretty well," I said once, but she only gave me an incredulous glance.

About twilight, I said to no one in particular, "Why do you suppose the silos are always on the same side of the road, and always about the same distance away?"

Ella pushed a loose strand of blond hair back

from her flushed forehead. "That's obviously where the railroad tracks are."

I asked her, where did she see any tracks?

"I didn't. I did not need to."

Behind us, there was a sharp crack and a yelp that sounded like David.

"It's his fault, Mom. I told him not to put his feet over here, but he keeps doing it."

Ella said a few quick words in German, which all of us understood and used from time to time, having long since discovered that the choice of language at any given moment could be a statement in itself.

The silence that followed seemed unusually peaceful, and it was a moment before I realized that the engine had stopped. Air rushed gently around the car as it gradually slowed. Ella moved the wheel a half inch, and we drifted to the side of the road.

Hank took his thumb out of his mouth and sat up. We all looked out the windows, as if our help would come from out there.

"*Weh mir,*" Charlie sighed.

I got out, looked at the engine, jiggled some wires, but it wouldn't start. I pushed, Ella clutched, and on the fourth try it started, but it didn't sound the same. Instead of a low steady purr, it hammered high and fast, dropped to a growl, gasped out some low putts.

Through the rest of Kansas, we stopped at every

gas station in every town. Men and boys looked at, in, under and around the Lancia, asked what it was, pushed their caps back with their thumbs and shook their heads.

"Could be the voltage regulator," one said. "Does it have one?" Another said, "Distributor's gone wrong."

"Denver," they all said. "Nobody around here's got the parts."

I was driving when we crossed the border into eastern Colorado. Around us, skull-bleaching sun hit shallow, morose-looking hills. The ground was littered with burnt stubble, as if it had been planted with something years before, then cut and left to dry out. It was a landscape that spoke of dinosaur death, indifferent to the lesser life forms passing over it since.

I watched a white silo loom up about a mile from the road, and it was nearly past when I realized that it was *on the right*.

"Hey," I said, watching it go by. "They've changed sides. Did you see any railroad tracks change sides? I sure as hell didn't."

In English, pronouncing all of the consonants in each word, Ella said, "Are you certain that you are going the right way?"

Covertly I searched for a road sign. A better man might have judged by the sun, but as far as I could tell it was centrally located and might have been headed in any direction. The rest of the sky was no help. It was a pale washed-out blue, broken only by a smirk of moon.

On the horizon was a low yellow fog.

❖❖❖

After the sheep, no amount of pushing would make the car start. I sat behind the wheel, resting. The car and I were now a couple of hundred yards closer to California than were Ella and the boys. Down the road about a mile I could see a clump of dark trees, three or four houses, and an abandoned gas station.

I walked back to where Ella was sitting on a mound of sand. Without looking at her I said I'd walk up to that settlement and see what I could find.

"Can I come?" Charlie shouted, clutching my pant leg, but I removed his hands and said, "No, damnit, I'm going alone." Instantly he started to cry again, and though I patted him on the back of the head and said, "Hey, I'm sorry, buddy, but look, it's too far," he wouldn't stop. Finally I walked away, without looking at anyone.

The closer I got to the settlement, the less promising it seemed. No dogs or children played in the yards, no wash flapped on the lines. The only vehicle I could see was a Model T, resting tireless in a sandy lot.

13

I reached the former gas station. The yard was unpaved, the old pumps orange with rust. The garage doors had been removed and the repair bays were crammed to the ceiling with old tires, rusted engines, broken fenders, road signs, used pipes and miscellaneous trash that must have been gathered over hundreds of miles of highway. On the dirty stucco wall the sign said SO 10, with an H of cleaner white stucco in the gap.

The weathered door of the office stood open, and I glanced inside. It was dark and cool and seemed surprisingly in order. There was a wooden counter with glass in the front, behind which lay three packs of Lucky Strikes. A hand-lettered sign nailed to the wall said *"Sorry No Telephone."*

On the counter was another note, printed in pencil on brown paper: "Be right back. Alf." Beside it was a brown paper bag, open at the top. Idly I leaned over and looked in. It was full of money — a wad of dollar bills, some loose tens and twenties, a couple of pounds of quarters and nickels and dimes.

I stepped out into the yard, shaded my eyes and looked east toward Ella and the boys, then west up the road. It occurred to me that a man hitching alone could take any ride that came along — trucks, tractors, travelling salesmen — and be in California before morning. He could sell his house and live in a tent and have beer with lunch every day for the rest of his life. The weather was mild there, I had heard, all the time, and the girls wore flimsy dresses that blew against their legs like springtime, all year round.

It wasn't that I didn't love my wife and children, I hastily assured myself — I did, and I wished them well. It was just that I could have been happy with less. I tried to explain it once to Ella, and I ended up saying I could have been happy as a note from a saxophone. It was the sort of thing that happened when she refused to see what I meant and I went farther and farther trying to tell her. On the other hand, I knew just the note: the first time I heard it, it was played by Coleman Hawkins, and another one, a lot like it, was by Lester Young. It started off low and nasty like a bray, but it kept on and got wide and tender and silty, and you could float on it till you forgot what was happening at all.

❖◈❖

A man came striding briskly up the highway from the west. His eyes fixed on me as he walked, and he turned into the station yard. He was stocky, looked about fifty, with dark suncracked skin. He had on a black baseball cap and brown clothes he had obviously slept in for a long time. His pants were stapled together along the seams. He gripped the brim of his cap and swirled it on his head, fanning his long hair evenly around.

"May I help you with something," he said, in a deep pleasant voice. It was pitched to carry no farther than my ear and was wrong for the way he looked. He sounded like someone you could meet in the common room of a house at Harvard, not like an unemployed sheepherder in stapled pants. He was also much younger than I had thought, more like my own age. I glanced at his clothes, wondering if they might be khaki fatigues. You could see faintly where the name tag had been ripped off, over the pocket.

"My car's stalled up the road."

"That one?" he said and pointed. "We'll push it up here." He took off striding up the highway.

I caught up, thanked him, and asked if he knew of a telephone nearby and how far it was to the nearest garage.

"What do you need?" He gazed up at me without squinting, out of clear green eyes.

I told him I had no idea and described what the car was doing.

"We could try charging the battery," he said evenly.

"Charging the — you mean you — back there? At the station?"

He didn't answer but kept walking toward the car. When we reached it, Ella and the boys were inside, Charlie and David trying to climb out the back windows onto the roof. Inching their fingers out onto the burning metal, they established their positions and looked at Ella. Sharply, in German, she told them to quit horsing around.

The man held out his arm, open palm over the car. "Let them stay inside. Would she mind steering?"

Ella looked at him suspiciously and pressed her lips together, climbing into the driver's seat. The boys turned and watched as the man and I pushed the car, tires crunching dully up the sandy flat along the side of the road.

"Brrrrrrrmmmmmm, brrrrrrrmmmmmmm," the man said. I turned and smiled at him, assuming he was doing it for the boys, though they couldn't hear him through the glass. But he wasn't looking at them. His expression was serious and calm, as if I had asked his advice on a weighty matter.

"Brrrrrrmmmmmm, brrrrrrmmmmmmm," he said. His mouth wound up through first, dropped into second, rose with a whine, dropped to third, and down-shifted for the turn into the station yard. "Screeeeeeeeeeeeee," he said, rearing back solemnly, putting on the brakes. The boys and I stared at him, but he didn't seem to mind.

"Over by the garage," he said. "A bit closer." We moved it back and forth several times before he was satisfied. He went into the office.

Ella and the boys got out of the car and stood looking around. "Do not touch that!" she said sharply in German, the moment the boys started for the garage. "Stay out of there!" She held on to their shoulders while they studied the pile of trash.

The man came out of the office carefully rolling a black box on a trolley. He pushed it up to the back of the car and steered it this way and that until it was in just the right position. He opened the hood and bent over the engine, then walked quickly around the side of the building, as if he'd forgotten something he needed.

Ella walked to the back of the car, and I followed her. We examined the box. It was roped together with twine, bare wire showing through the leads, which were patched with masking tape. It was not hooked up to the car. The battery was in plain sight, and he had left a pair of pliers on the fender.

"I'm sure he'll be right back," I said, but ten minutes later he had not returned, and the battery charger was still not connected to the car.

She took me over to the garage and pointed. "Look at this." Embedded in the mass of trash, wedged in tight, were three crates of Coke. I got closer and, sure enough, they were capped bottles, full of black liquid and furred with dust. All three cases were so deep in that not a single bottle could have been extracted.

"So what," I said, though I have to admit the sight worried me. If this was Alf, writer of the note and owner of the brown bag of money, wasn't he in some kind of business here, which might involve the selling of Coke? There was an old red cooler by the office door. Casually I leaned on it, and it hummed into my hand. I lifted the lid. It was cold inside, but empty. Beads of ice water were being kept well chilled.

I strolled around to the back of the building, where a door stood open, letting out a smell of pine cleanser. Inside was a large bathroom, recently white-washed, with a clean white roller towel. Alf was putting a new roll of toilet paper into the rack, and doing it with such dignity and care that I ducked out of his line of sight and pressed myself against the wall of the building. In front of me, across a field of thistles, was a shack, nailed together out of weathered boards, burlap bags hanging over the windows and doorway.

I sneaked back around to the station yard, where Ella was struggling with David and Charlie, who wanted to climb the trash in the garage. Hank was standing with buckled knees, feet wide apart, leaning on the station wall and pointing to something over his head. I picked him up. He reached out and didn't quite touch a gray papery wasp's nest on the wall.

"Bee's house," I said, and he watched my mouth.

A loose sheet of newspaper blew across the station yard just as Alf came around the corner. He caught it, smoothed it out, folded it into a square. He went over to our car, bent over it briefly, then returned to the back of the building.

I walked over and took a look. The leads were attached to the battery, and the two dials on the box were registering, but at different levels.

A new Cadillac turned off the highway and rolled in, crunching gravel, misled by the sight of our car. A big red-faced man sat looking toward the office. Beside him a fat woman with pink arms turned and said something sharp to the children in the back seat. The driver gave a blast of his mighty horn, glanced at me, then blasted his horn again. He backed out and drove away.

Alf came around the side of the building with a brown bag in his arms and went into the office. A moment later he walked over to where I was standing and looked up at me.

"The children are hungry, aren't they? It isn't much, but if you'll bring them into the office —"

"Oh," I said, startled. "You don't need to —" I stopped, seeing his quietly eager look. "Why, sure. That's kind of you. Thanks."

I approached Ella cautiously, not sure why I thought it was all right. "He keeps a beautiful bathroom," I said lamely.

She gave me such a lost look, as if she no longer hoped for help, that I nearly reached for her. I too was picturing us sleeping in the car, flagging down trucks to beg for food, though I wouldn't have admitted it. She turned away abruptly, called sharply to the boys. I went into the office.

Alf was behind the counter, leaning on his arms, waiting. On the counter were three small jars of water and five sandwiches on a white china plate. They were neatly sliced on the diagonal, white bread and what looked like peanut butter and grape jelly.

"They're washing their hands," I said.

He nodded and watched out the window for them. While we waited, another car drove up to the pumps and the driver looked toward the office, but Alf did not move. The car was still waiting when Ella came through the door warily, peering into the dark, holding Hank on one hip and David by the hand.

Alf clutched his cap, swirled it around on his head. "*Bitte,*" he said and gestured with his palm toward the three stools in front of the counter. "*Sich hinsetzen, bitte.*"

Ella and I stared at him in astonishment. He continued to gaze back at us calmly. "*Sich hinsetzen, bitte, gnädige Frau. Und der Kinder. Essen, bitte.*"

I lifted Charlie and David onto stools and took Hank from Ella. She sat down. Alf held the plate toward her, and slowly she took a sandwich.

"*Danke. Sehr freundlich von Ihnen!*" she said, watching him.

He gave her an urgent look. "*Essen. Bitte, essen.*"

He held the plate for each of us, including Hank, who only stared at him. Ella reached up and took one for him.

"Forgiveness," Alf said in German and glanced at me. "Only three glasses." He put the plate down and eased out around the counter. "*Essen. Bitte.*" He walked briskly out to the car that was still waiting at the pumps, swirling his hair around with his cap.

We all sat completely still, holding our sandwiches, watching Alf. He cranked up one of the rusty pumps and inserted the nozzle into the car's tank.

"He cannot have any gasoline?" Ella whispered.

I shrugged. I was thinking about Alf's German and the places he could have learned it, where they didn't do much eating, or much apologizing. Four summers before, I had ridden home from Europe on a ship full of men who had been prisoners of war. The ones who didn't have typhus went on regular troopships, though they weren't allowed to eat with us, since their stomachs couldn't take regular rations yet. They were nothing but eyes and cheekbones, and most of them didn't move out of their bunks, but when we docked in New York the rest of us hung back and let them clear off first, and we saw them all go down the plank. There must have been a thousand women on the dock below, and they all

22

seemed to have on new hats, red hats, dark blue, yellow, green, gray, brown, white, with feathers and veils, and they all went silent while those men went down. By the time it was over they sounded like a crowd again, and when it was my turn to slant down into those hats, all I could think about was how much I wanted Ella not to speak to me in German.

Alf leaned over, picked up a bucket and took out a rag. Slowly and carefully he polished the car's windshield. He did the side windows, the back, and the outside mirrors. When he was finished, he took hold of the nozzle and topped off the tank. The driver gave him some money, and just as the car was pulling away, another one drove in.

We ate the sandwiches and drank the water. The boys got down and wandered into the yard, and we went out to watch them.

A car pulling a large silver trailer rolled into the station yard and parked at the pumps. Alf put in the nozzle and washed the windows on the car. He walked to the garage, got a wooden crate and stood on it to clean the windows of the trailer.

"That's okay," said the guy who owned the trailer. "You don't need to do that."

Alf didn't seem to hear him. He worked slowly, rinsing after he washed, scraping off little imperfections with his fingernail. When he finished a window, he got down and moved the crate into just the right position under the next one.

"Hey, that's okay," the trailer man said.

Two more cars rolled in and started waiting. A man in a cowboy hat parked his pickup by the office, got out and stood beside it, watching Alf.

Alf stepped down from the crate and walked briskly behind the building without saying a word to anyone. The three men who were waiting stuck their chins out, squinting toward where he had gone. The owner of the trailer studied the gas nozzle, which was still in his car.

Instinctively I spread out my arms, as if to attract their attention. Fellow travellers! I wanted to cry out. Do not be alarmed. He will be back. Is it so essential to move unerringly from A to B, without an occasional sidetrip to J or X? Won't you arrive the richer at B, for those bits of Q? We are coded for incomprehensibility. Confusion is as much a part of truth as chart and diagram.

Five minutes later he was still not back. The man who owned the trailer removed the nozzle from his car, got in and started the engine. Before I realized what was happening, Ella rushed up to the car window.

"That will be one dollar and forty-nine cents,"

she said, loudly and firmly. There was no price posted on the pump, but it showed how much had gone in, and she must have multiplied fast, using the going rate from other stations.

The driver stared at her with his lips parted, then smiled and took out his wallet. I went over to the other car waiting at the pump. It was a new Buick, the driver a heavy man in a red Hawaiian shirt. I asked what he'd have.

"You got gas in those?" He gestured with his thumb.

I assured him that we did, cranked up the pump and stuck the nozzle in his tank. At first when I squeezed the handle nothing happened, but then I felt the cold rush as the gas came up from underground, and the smell hit my nose. A shimmer like heat wavered over the opening to the tank.

When it was full, Ella was there with the figures. "One eighty-three," she said to the driver, took his money, and handed it to me. She gave me a bland steady look. Cautiously I smiled at her. I moved on to the next car.

Finally Alf came back and went into the office. The man in the cowboy hat followed. When I went in to give him the money, he was counting out bills from the brown paper sack. He handed them to the man in the cowboy hat.

"Much obliged," said the cowboy hat. "You'll get it back Monday."

Alf ripped a small piece off the paper sack and wrote something down. When I gave him the money from the three cars, he tore off another piece and wrote down that amount. He put the little pieces of paper in a neat stack on the counter.

◇•◇•◇

It was getting late, the pumps throwing long shadows, when Alf disconnected the charger. He rolled it into the office. I went in and sat on a stool.

He was leaning on the counter. He looked at me as if he was glad I was there and felt we didn't need to talk. We both looked out the window at the yard. I asked what did I owe him.

"You don't owe me anything."

"You mean, because I helped you out? That was just for something to do. What about the electricity?"

He made a neater stack of his pieces of paper. "Couldn't have been more than a nickel."

I gave him a nickel. He put it in the bag and wrote something on a brown paper wafer.

I asked him how far it was to Denver.

"It's a hundred and twelve miles to Denver. You might make it before dark if you don't have any more trouble."

I thanked him and went out to the car. The boys

26

were inside, and Ella was sitting in the driver's seat, holding Hank. I got in, and she handed him to me. For a moment, nobody moved.

"Ready?" she said, and I nodded.

She pushed the ignition. The car started, and it ran smoothly all the way to Denver.

ODE TO JOY

MAYBE IT WAS TAKING off her nightgown, at that particular minute — she should have waited until Edward was gone. So what if Hank crawled at autobahn speed. So what if he would be out the door and into the street. It didn't matter if David liked to jab little toys into electric sockets, and if lately Charlie had discovered death. Worms could be impaled, he'd found, ants drowned in spit. He liked to catch his little brothers, seal their mouths with a chubby palm and watch what happened, face composed with a scientist's calm. She could have lined them up, made them sing, something Charlie liked, a German animal song: "Snail, snail, look out, snail, I'm going to grab you and throw you in a ditch!" He would swing his hands to that, smash down a handful of air. Three times through would have been enough, she'd be in her clothes. Instead she dove at Edward as he raced for the door.

"Wait! Five minutes — please?"

On the floor, David and Charlie knelt next to Tinkertoy towers, wearing Superman pajamas, red capes askew. Their heads tracked Edward as he passed, like dandelions turned toward the sun. He was dressed to teach, in a tweed jacket, clean shirt, creased flannel pants. He did it alone, with the door closed, rehearsing his lecture while perfecting his tie.

"You will watch them? Three minutes!"

He didn't appear to hear, but he perched on the arm of the couch, unfolding his notes. Hands trembling slightly, he held the yellow sheets toward the light from the window. It was his first year of teaching at Berkeley, and he woke up sweating before a lecture. Tonight his shirt would reek like goat rut, and he'd drink two fast martinis. He would tell her things he'd said, things that had come to him in the middle of the lecture: "The universe was constructed on the principle of jazz (if you make a mistake, don't take it back, repeat it)." "To say 'I love you' is to join three indeterminate terms." His face would be skeptical, slightly amused, as if he'd been listening to somebody else. Then he would think of something he shouldn't have said. What did Thoreau mean about the man who ate nothing but carrots? a student had asked. "Live by big ideas and you turn orange," he said to that. What about space, time and relativity in modern art? "What a name for a horse!"

He'd lean on the table, push both hands through his hair. He was a fraud, he was no philosopher, he should resign. He wouldn't be hungry, he'd just pace hollow-eyed. She'd have to go to bed, to be ready for the boys at dawn. If she got up to look for him in the night, he might have left the house. Already he knew graduate students who would meet him anytime, drink until the bars closed down. They'd wander the streets, shouting and arguing, end up with a pilgrimage to Isadora Duncan's former house, and he'd come home with a raw throat, clothes wet from the morning fog. He invented a drink, whiskey and Cheracol, and called it Isadora's Scarf.

"Edward! Watch Hank. Please?"

He only raised his eyebrows. Robe half off, she paused in the doorway, looking back. David and Charlie had given up waiting for him to notice them, and they sat listlessly, chins down, nudging Tinker-toys around with limp fingers. Across the room, Hank spied his father. Dropping to all fours, he trotted across the rug, stopped at his feet. Rearing up unsteadily, diaper sagged out of rubber pants, he gripped a shoelace on the hard brown shoes and leaned back, small arm straight and high, undoing the bow, eyes wide with awe and delight.

From the radio a boy's voice piped. "Hi, I'm Buster Brown, I live in a shoe!"

Charlie's face lit tentatively. "I'm Buster Poo, I live in a shoepoo."

Without looking down, Edward removed Hank's fingers from his shoe. Hank watched him, smiling. He reached for the half-knot and pulled that out, too.

The moment seemed right. Sweeping the nightgown over her head, she ran to the bedroom, threw open the closet, fingered for a dress.

Out in the living room, the older boys squealed softly. "I'm Buster Poopoo, I live in a poopoopoo!"

Nothing was clean — nothing but narrow wartime waists, nothing she had been able to button since Edward came back. Where was the blue-check dress?

From the radio, a deep male voice. "Twang your magic twanger, Froggy!"

"Poo your magic pooper, Poopoo!"

"Pee your magic peepoo, Poopie!"

She ran to the hamper, pawed through small corduroy overalls, tiny balled socks, Edward's sour shirts. From the living room came happy shrieks.

"Poo your magic poopoo, Peepee!"

"Pee your magic peepeepoopookaka!"

"Poopoopeepeekakapeepeepoopookakapoopoo-poopoopeepeepeepeekakakakakakakaka!"

Edward, disgusted. "All right. That's enough of that."

The blue-check dress was at the bottom of the hamper, milk crusted down the front. She held it up, listening to footsteps in the living room, murmurs from David and Charlie. *Thump* went something heavy and soft, like a baby's head.

"Ella," Edward said dully. His voice shot up an octave. He was screaming. "Ella!"

She clutched her robe, but it caught on the hook and tore. She let it go and ran. David and Charlie were on the floor, but she couldn't see Hank. Edward stood at the window, shrieking. The window was open and had no screen, and below it was a long drop past the garage to the street.

"Where is he?" she yelled, trying to see out the window. Why did Edward refuse to move out of the way? Hank was not dangling out, not dead on the sidewalk. She dashed to the kitchen, to the hallway.

"Ella!" Edward screamed, with a deep note like rage. He went on standing at the window.

She ran to the boys' room, to their own room, though she knew he couldn't be there, she was in there when it happened.

"Edward!" She ran back to the living room. "Tell me where he is!"

"Help me!" He was hoarse with panic and accusation.

She focussed on him. His face was twisted and red, eyes wide and white. He was very tall, but he seemed almost to dangle from the window — both hands caught in the frame. He must have tried to open it with his fingertips curled over the top of the sash and smashed them into the crossbar of the upper panes, at the same time reaching the place where the window stuck, going crooked in its runners, and he didn't know how to pull it down. The cottage was old, with buckled floors, doorbolts that no longer met their holes, and all the windows stuck when raised or dropped unexpectedly like guillotines. After six months, she knew exactly what it took to close each one. Why didn't he?

Stepping up to the window, she felt the breeze stir her pubic hair. Plucking the drape, she tried to pull it in front of her, but it slipped back to the side when she reached for the window. Edward screamed all the while. She had to stand square in the window to get both hands on top of the sash, and she did it in a rush — knocked it straight, pulled it down.

"My God!" he shrieked, leaping away. "You pushed it up!"

She ran to the closet for her robe. Charlie was crying his particularly irritating cry, nagging and raucous. The other two had sweet cries, you wanted to pick them up right away, but not Charlie — his was a raw demand. Running past, she paused to put her hand on his head, but he pulled it away.

"Where is Hank?" she yelled. He wasn't in the kitchen. She ran back to the living room. "Where is Hank?"

Edward was lying on the couch, hands up like the paws of a dead mouse. He turned his head slowly to stare at her, as if he saw letters a hundred feet high coming up over the horizon. She held her robe closed. The torn flap in back let cold air in on her skin. "Your son Hank. The one that is missing. Do you remember him?"

He held up his hands, fingers trembling. Some of the nails were purple and split, oozing blood. His voice was quiet. "Do me a favor. Next time I need help, call the fire department."

She ran to the bedrooms, searched the hallway. She ran to the front door. "Can I avoid it if you don't know how to open a window?"

She ran out into the yard. Yellow sunshine lit the grass, flowers frothed pink and white. Hank was nowhere. He was lost. The cement steps were cold on her bare feet. She ran down the block, searched other people's yards. She stepped on a stone, bruised her heel, had to run on her toes. Hank was nowhere. She ran back to the house.

David and Charlie were kneeling by the couch, eyes dark with grief. Edward ignored them, lying like a corpse in state. Edward had lost him, Edward, who had once lost his paycheck, who emptied burning pipe coals into trash. Once he had even lost her. It was before the boys were born, when they still lived in Cambridge and Edward was in graduate school at Harvard. One frozen February night, their car stalled in the middle of Boston, and he went off to call a tow truck. When he came back, he couldn't find the car, so he decided she had fixed it and left without him. He took the subway home. The tow truck didn't find her either, and she waited four hours in the unheated car. Privately, under her coat, she urinated into a jar. Finally, after midnight, she called their apartment. "Where've you been?" Edward snarled, safe and warm. "Where exactly have you been this time?"

She crouched beside him, as he lay on the couch. She whispered in German — she had taught the boys a little, but not much. She had not taught them the words for "criminal irresponsibility," "child murder," or the word "divorce."

Edward opened his eyes but did not look at her. "Promise?"

"Oh, you would like that, I know. No responsibilities, no demands. Nothing but your own selfishness. Well, I'd make sure you never saw the boys again." It was inside Edward's ears before she realized she was going to say it.

"Oh, really." He swung his big brown shoes to the floor and sat up, jabbing the air near her chest with the backs of his hands. She backed away.

"They'll go with me — won't you, boys? And I'll tell them all about selfishness. I'll tell them how you've used me, and used me up. We'll discuss it at some length, the boys and I — emotional selfishness, and sexual. Especially sexual. Women's sexual selfishness, that'll be a big point with us, with me and my sons. I'll make sure they understand that, while they're growing up. With me. You want to come with me, don't you?"

Kneeling on the floor, they stared at him. He gripped their shoulders with big bleeding hands.

"Don't you? Don't you want to come with me?"

Charlie let out a low cry, rising like a fire siren. But he was nodding. Edward scooped him up in one arm, David in the other, pressed them to his chest. Charlie hung rigid, fists in his eyes, crying high thin notes, but David clung with arms and knees, and Edward could let him go, free a hand to open the door. They were in the sun, down the steps, into the street.

She was right behind him in her bare feet, voice quiet, soothing. "For the sake of God, Edward. Edward. Do not do this."

She ran on her toes, just behind him, keeping one palm on David's back. He wasn't crying but his eyes were huge and round. "Okay. Edward. Put them down now."

If she did not hit him or scream or threaten, the panic would leave him, he would put them down. Once he had leaped out of a moving car, saying he didn't want to be married to her anymore. He ran up an alley and disappeared. When she found him, sitting in the snow in Harvard Yard, he wept and said he couldn't live without her. Sometimes he threw things — plates, books, pens, once a bottle of ink. If she kept quiet, didn't yell back, he would clean up what was broken, wipe the ink off the walls. He'd rest his head on her shoulder and apologize. "Another triumph of the human spirit," he'd sigh.

He ran across the street to the car. Charlie was sliding down around his waist. He had to take his hand off David to hunch Charlie up to his shoulder, and she got an arm around David's waist, pulled him away. Pressing his small body to her hip, she ran for the house.

As she made the stairs she heard Edward's shoes grinding grit behind her. Glancing back, she saw him towering, horrible face, jacket wings flying wide. His fingers dug into her shoulders.

"Two out of four, you'd settle for that, wouldn't you? Put us in neat numbered packages, take out two at a time and train us exactly the way you want, little perfect goddamn cuckoo clocks that do exactly —"

"Edward, Edward," she was saying all the while.

He pressed her against the wall of the house and leaned over her, weight all on one foot. He stared down at her, his eyes flat and black, without expression. Suddenly he had David. They were out in the street, into the car. The engine started, rose to a roar, receded down the hill.

❖❖❖

Overhead a mockingbird was imitating lawn mowers, jackhammers, doorbells, other birds. *Chirrrrrup!* it said. *Chirr chirr chirr chirr rack rack rack rackety rack. Rookety rookety rookety rack rack rack! Be sweet! Be sweet! Be sweet! Be sweet!* Along the walkway, irises unfurled their tight torpedoes. The sun warmed her dark robe the same as the grass, the wall, the concrete.

No woman of her family since the beginning of time had ever lost a child. Her older sister, Pia, had gotten four out of Berlin in 1945, on foot. Pia had refused to go with the rest of the family when they left the country. Ella didn't want to go either, because she had just been picked to train for the Berlin Olympics, and the Swiss didn't have a good swim team. But she was too young to say no, and she had to go with her parents to Basel, where a few years later she met Edward, on his junior year abroad, and followed him home.

She hadn't seen anyone in her family since. She supposed that Pia must have become a Nazi. Pia married an officer in the SS and had four children before he was killed on the eastern front. The oldest was no bigger than Charlie at the end of the war, and she had to carry two of them. Pia told the story to their mother, who wrote it to Ella. She said she took along a pistol to shoot the children with, and herself, if they were caught by the Russians. She walked west, with nothing to eat, and she made it to the American army, with all four children still alive.

Angrily an engine forged up the hill, jerked to a stop. Metal doors creaked, hard shoes grated. Ella put up her hands as Edward lowered David in a tight ball, knees to chest, hands in fists. His red cape was gone.

Charlie stood in the street, crying. Edward lifted him to his chest and stood motionless, head tipped back, eyes closed. Without changing his posture, he turned toward the house. He tested each step before putting his weight down, as if Charlie were asleep. He stepped around her, climbed the stairs to the house. He came back out alone, walked quickly to the car and drove away.

Charlie lay on the couch, plucking a thread on

his pajamas. He had stopped crying. She carried David in and sat beside him. The house was so still they could hear the refrigerator buzz.

After a while, Charlie nudged David with his heel. He lay smirking, chin hunched on his chest, eyes slightly crossed. "She doesn't have a peepee at all," he whispered, looking satisfied. "She sits down to go wee."

Bathroom, she thought, and shot off the couch. The door was closed, half-hidden behind the door to the boys' room, and she'd run past it, again and again.

Carefully she opened it and groped for the light. The tile floor was littered with white ruffles. Leaning on the wall, reaching up on tiptoe, Hank was unrolling toilet paper onto the floor. When the light came on, he arched his whole spine, turning to look up at her. Thin sheets of tissue were pressed between his lips. Grinning shyly, he dropped his gaze and patted the roll, humming a contented monotone.

◆◇◆

The light was clear yellow, like a Vermeer, on streets so empty they might have been evacuated. In other cities you could see women on the streets, watching out the windows, coming and going from little shops. But in Berkeley there was too much space, everyone lived in a separate house, moated with yard, and no one walked, everyone drove cars. Lone-liness came in the window like the ocean air. Stand-ing on a chair, unhooking the drapes, she could see details on the campanile, kilometers away: pale stone against dark trees, arches opening to a blue pure as ether, and not a human form in sight.

She folded the drapes. They were long and heavy, dark blue and figured with white waves, like a Japanese print, and much too formal for the little crooked cottage. She had made them herself during the war, without a machine, using thousands of tiny hand-stitches. She had lined them to the floor, sewn triangular weights in the hems, and matched every fine line of the pattern along all twelve meters of seam. No one would ever notice the perfection of those seams, but she had never regretted that she'd done them right.

She took the mattress out of the big black pram and put the drapes in its place. Over them she smoothed two layers of cotton diapers, a rubber crib sheet, and more diapers. Pia, of course, would not have needed to take those. In the only picture she had of her, Pia was giving a violin recital, in a black dress with her hair swept up, and Ella usually imagined her walking out of Berlin like that, carrying her violin, her children walking calmly in clean clothes, even the baby, walking calmly, holding hands, without a diaper. When Charlie was born, Pia had sent her instructions for toilet training. Start at six months, she said. Hold him over the toilet and speak to him sternly. Did she want to become a soft American?

"So that's how they make Nazis," Edward said. But when he wasn't home, she secretly tried it. Charlie couldn't say a word yet, but he had given her such a scandalized look, such a stare of disillusionment and indictment, that she stopped at once. He seemed never to have forgotten it. She didn't try again until he was two, but the whole experience seemed seared into his brain. These days, he seldom talked about anything else.

"You poopoohead!" he yelled at David, as they jockeyed for the front of the pram in their blue shorts suits. "You kakapeepeepoopoohead!"

He launched himself at it, like a salmon up a waterfall, and managed to flop over the side rail. David caught his bare knees, screaming. "Mom! Mom!"

She got them down, lined them up. There would be rules, she said. No fighting, no standing up, no whining in the pram. Anyone who did forfeited his turn in front, and because Charlie had started that fight, David would ride there first, for half an hour. She showed them the tiny face of her watch — it had been her grandmother's, with rubies in the corners almost too small to see. It was the only valuable thing she owned, besides her engagement ring, and she was wearing that, too.

She changed Hank one last time and left the dirty diapers in the pail, wondering how long it would be before Edward noticed them. She let the older boys climb into the pram and put in their lunch. At the last moment she ran through the house, looking at dishes, at pictures, at things she could not take. Hank would hardly fit in the pram now.

"Poopoopoo-pooperding!" David crowed, leaning forward like a figurehead on a ship, holding the gunwales and rocking. Charlie sulked against the bulkhead, Hank between his knees, as far as possible from David. "Poopoopoo-pooperslooper!"

Leaning into the chrome rail, she launched the overloaded pram. The hill was steep, and soon she had to lean back, gripping the rail and half-running on her toes. One wheel let out a squeal almost too high to hear. The boys' fine hair was light as kitten down, and the breeze flipped it straight up off their foreheads, exposing solemn baby faces.

❖❖❖

They reached the bank in fifteen minutes but had to wait in line. Ahead of them, a little boy stood holding his mother's hand, twisting around to stare at the boys in the pram.

Charlie leaned out toward him, murmuring confidentially. "My mother doesn't have a peepee. She sits down to go wee." He hunched down in the pram, giggling hard, palm over his mouth. The little boy flopped around blindly, pressed his face into his mother's knees.

"All but ten dollars," she told the teller, avoiding her eyes. She had resolved to take all the money, but there was less than three hundred, and even if she took it all, it wouldn't get them past New York. She'd have to be careful, spend as little as possible. She counted the bills twice, folded them into her pocket.

Their next stop was a school in East Oakland, where she changed Hank's diaper. She rinsed out the wet one and hung it over the struts beneath the pram. They were near the bay now, and as they left the playground, they passed weathered wooden houses, crowded together. Negro men idled in groups, smoking, gray hats pulled low over their foreheads.

"Mom!" Charlie pointed urgently, whispering. "Mom! Who are all these garbagemen?"

"Stop your mouth. Do not say anything to them."

"Hello," she said to the men. She walked firmly but not too fast. In the silence she could hear the pram wheels squeak. "Hello. Good morning."

In the pram the boys stared rudely, lips parted.

A few men nodded. As a girl she had passed crowds like these, German men but just like them, smoking, empty-eyed, shadows around the bones in their cheeks. She was afraid of them, but Pia had told her to be quiet. Those men had no jobs, she said, and prices doubled every day — they had fought in the war, and now they had to steal to get bread for their families. Hello, Pia said to them. Good morning, hello, while the men appraised their coats, their stockings, their gloves. Their father was in the government, and it didn't matter to them that prices kept going up.

"Hello. Good morning," she said.

She turned a corner, hoping to see the highway. Instead she saw a large and silent group of men, standing all over a front lawn and blocking the sidewalk.

"Excuse me," she said, pushing the pram into the crowd. Slowly the men moved aside. Some murmured politely, but most kept silent. She could feel their stares on the back of her neck.

They were just leaving the crowd, heading into open sidewalk, when suddenly Charlie turned and shrilled back to them. "My mother does not have a peepee!"

"Silence," she hissed, walking faster.

He half stood up, clutching the rails. "She doesn't have one at all!"

A chorus of chuckles swelled, rolling over them like a benediction.

❖·❖·❖

At last she could see the highway. Beyond it rose the Bay Bridge, like an intricate steel trap above the water. Briskly she walked by the trolley station. Twenty-one cents was all it cost, all the way to San Francisco, and it must be fifteen kilometers across. She knew she should take it, that it would make sense, and that she wasn't going to. It was eighty-four cents she did not have to spend, and the pram wouldn't fit through the doors — she'd be holding Hank, the curtains, the lunch, the diapers, without a free hand for the older boys. She wanted to do it alone, without help. She knew it might be foolish, but it was instinctive, even animal, and she wasn't going to argue with it. When a cat moved its kittens to a more secret place, it held them in its mouth and ran, with challenging eyes. She didn't want to discuss it with anyone.

She took the bypass under the highway, and the frontage road along the mudflats. Across the water, halfway to the horizon, a white cloud hid the Golden Gate. Just in front of her, the Bay Bridge stretched to the city's low white towers. It was a long bridge, in two parts, broken by an island. The trolley did not stop at Yerba Buena, and the roadway passed

46

through a tunnel — the island was closed to civilians. Attached to it, stretched out flat along the water, was an armored strip of landfill called Treasure Island, lately used for fighting the war in the Pacific.

No one was allowed to visit Treasure Island, and yet she, Ella, had once lived on it for three weeks. During the war, she lived alone in Cambridge while Edward was away on a ship. She hadn't seen him for close to a year when she got a letter saying "holes in his socks." He had so many holes in his socks, the letter said, he was afraid they'd fall apart, at the latest by the fifteenth. "A lingering cough" meant Seattle, and "drinking too much" was San Diego. The codes for the east coast were completely different, from his studies: "epistemological circle," "subjective sublime," and "essentialist ideal." Holes in his socks meant San Francisco.

She left Boston that night, waited days for a connecting train in Chicago and again in Denver, but on the twelfth she arrived in San Francisco, where she was arrested as a German spy. The other passengers on the train had done their patriotic duty, and now the FBI did theirs. They impounded Edward's letters, cracked the codes, and questioned her every day, politely disbelieving everything she said. They kept her in a locked house with three officers in the WAVES, who stopped talking when she entered a room and left a ten-cent jar of deodorant on her bed.

It was weeks before Edward knew where she was, his ship having long since come and gone from "essentialist ideal."

◆◆◆◆

Somewhere down the highway a siren whined. Ducking into the parking lot beside the toll plaza, she sailed across toward water, as if to get a better view. A blue police car fled wailing by. The safest place would be just behind it. Running across the parking lot, she nosed the pram out onto the bridge.

"BLAAAAAAAAHHHHH," a car horn blasted, close beside her. "BLAAAAAAAAAHHHHH."

Some drivers were very excited: they braked elaborately, rolled down windows and yelled. It was true, the bridge had no sidewalk, but there was plenty of room in the extra space provided for mending tires. Charlie hunched fearfully, gripping the rails and staring back over his shoulder at the cars. Hank tried to climb out of the pram. Over and over she ordered him back, and he whined fitfully, kicking at David, who held him, staring ahead as if he'd lost all feeling in his arms.

"Do not worry," she called over the noise and walked as fast as she could.

Cars honked, braked, roared around them. Gradually the road tipped up. On the bay cloud-shadows skimmed across blue water, revealing its

48

true color, milky green. Every step lifted them higher, above cold water, into the wind.

They crested the arch of the first span, where the air was chill, shadowed by a lacework of steel. A needle of siren was piercing toward her. In the last stretch before the island, the bridge sloped down. She started running for the tunnel. Higher and higher it arched overhead, opening like a maw.

The siren was right behind them. She could see now inside the tunnel: the road narrowed, and there was no room along the side. But just before the entrance, where the bridge met the island, was a gate. Beyond it a field sloped away, down to the water.

She ran up to the gate. It was padlocked, high as her shoulders. Reaching through the bars, she set David and Charlie on the ground.

A blue police car pushed its chrome nose almost into her thigh. Holding Hank on one hip, she tried to heave the pram up to the top of the gate, but it crashed down on its side, tearing her stocking. She put one foot on it, the other on the gate. By the time she touched ground she was running, Hank wobbling on her hip. "Come on! Come on!"

The boys ran as if under fire.

◆◇◆◇◆

"Poo," David said, in three syllables, impressed. He and Charlie were kneeling beside her, watching as she took off Hank's diaper. They were hiding in a copse of live oak and chaparral, fronds of eucalyptus high above. Beyond the trees was a steep meadow, where long new grass was rippling, wind running down it like a herd of silver lemmings, into the bay.

She carried Hank down to the water and held him over it. Little waves lapped glittering under him, he squirmed and laughed. She dipped him in, to wash his bottom, and he gasped at the cold.

She looked at him sternly. "Peepee poopoo. Now, please."

He arched his back and squealed in protest.

"Please, Hank. Peepee poopoo. Please."

He threw back his head, wailing, and nearly broke her hold — he was too heavy. She dried him on the grass. She took off her blouse, pinned it around his bottom, and put her suit jacket back on, rough wool against her skin.

"I'm hungry," Charlie barked. David didn't say anything, but he watched her with bright eyes.

She told them lunch would be delayed. She told them to take hold of her skirt and to walk quietly. She set off across the meadow, toward the southern side of the island. Charlie was crying, clutching her skirt, one fist in his eye. David and Hank both watched him, eyes swelling, wet and round.

They crested a rise. Below them was a row of large white houses, officers' quarters for Treasure

Island. Out one back window a large orange-haired woman was watching them, and between the houses she could see a white jeep moving past, two men in uniform sitting up straight. Their heads were not turned her way, and she stepped into the shadow of a large tree. It was a fig tree, and green fruit oozing milk littered the ground. She glanced down at Charlie and David, sure they would refuse to step on anything so soft, but they both plodded over the figs as if they had ceased to notice their surroundings.

"This way," she said quietly, when she was sure the jeep was gone. She opened the gate at the back of the orange-haired woman's yard. Their feet sank into deep gravel between well-tended beds of flowers. As they approached the house, Ella looked up at the woman, who abruptly pulled down the windowshade.

They went out the front gate, across the lawn and down the sidewalk. They were an officer's wife, an officer's sons, strolling perhaps a bit too fast past landscaped lawns, across the island toward the main gate.

Near the entry to the bridge, a young sentry stood outside a guardhouse, gold braid looped around his shoulder as if to tie him up. Briskly she approached him, and he brought his heels together. "Good morning, ma'am," he said.

She nodded and smiled, continuing down the

51

sidewalk as if she meant to visit the lighthouse. At the last moment, in plain sight of the guard, she lurched onto the bridge.

This span was more open, airy as a harp, steel strings shining in sunlight. Car horns drowned all other sound, but as she became accustomed to it, it seemed like peace. A sea gull soared below them, keeping pace. A fresh breeze cooled their necks. Two cars pulled in front of them and stopped, a blue police car and a white jeep.

❖❖❖

"Everyone knows that, Charlie, sweetheart," Marcelline said. She picked a flake of tobacco off the end of her tongue. "Everyone knows that about your momma. That's why she's your momma, sweetheart, and not your daddy. No need to be telling that to people all the time."

Marcelline worked for the navy, but she did not exactly have on a uniform, just a white blouse and a dark skirt. Her desk was outside the small room where Ella and the boys had been sitting for three hours, since her interview with the FBI. Marcelline had brought them food and even, after a short delay, a diaper. Ella wasn't sure what she did, but she was too friendly to be a WAVE. Besides, she was a Negro, and all of the WAVES she had seen here the last time were white.

Ella had never actually talked to a Negro person before, but Marcelline seemed happy to talk to her. She would come into the room, sit on a hard wooden chair, light one fat cigarette after another, and talk. She was skinny and very tall, with large bulging eyes. Her hair was not curly but straight, light-brown and standing out around her head, like a mushroom cap. She was not married, but she was engaged to a Harlem Globetrotter, and they had two sons, slightly older than David and Charlie. Her best friend also had two babies by this man, but they were not engaged. Marcelline showed Ella the large yellow diamond on her hand.

She leaned forward and put a hand on Ella's arm. "You're no spy, now, are you." She chuckled. "Course you're not. With this many babies, this small? You don't have time to spy on your own self, leastwise anybody else. What do they think, you're going to care about giving secrets to the Russians?" She blew out smoke contemptuously. "No woman ever cared about a thing like that."

Ella half-smiled, watching her carefully. Of course she might be FBI — it would be a smart thing for them to do. They had not been satisfied with what she'd said: she was losing her German, she used it so little, she hardly talked to anyone but her husband, who spoke English. But if she was leaving her husband, they wanted to know, why did she not take the trolley, or the ferry, or the bus? Why did she try to walk through a restricted area? She had studied physics in college, and now she lived in walking distance of Berkeley's nuclear labs. Why had she not applied to be a U.S. citizen, when she'd been here eleven years? Where exactly was she going in Switzerland, and why?

Marcelline lit another cigarette, shook her head. "Now, I'm not saying it wouldn't be different, if there was some way you could throw yourself on into it. You know what I mean? If you could get yourself into an ecstasy of spying. Women have got to have the ecstasy —" She half-closed her eyes, lightly touching Ella's arm. "Don't they though? And most times that means two things, religion or love. You have to laugh at people like my mother and my sister — Rollers, they are. Out in the spirit every Saturday night, and looking forward to it all the rest of the week. But you and me, now, we're no different — don't say we're not. Every one of us's got lovesongs rising up to our mouths like bodies in a lake. We all just want a chance to pull our teeth out for God, or some man. We want to knock ourselves out, lay on out in some tomb and wait for Romeo to come down and wake us up. Walking your feet off for love is just a new variation."

Ella smiled politely and didn't bother to correct

her. She was thinking about the FBI. She supposed they were investigating her parents and calling Edward. She wondered how much they would tell him, but it wouldn't take much — by now he'd be sorry for the morning. He had probably been calling the cottage all afternoon, frantic to talk to her, and now that he knew where she was, he'd be on his way. She knew how he would come, driving so fast the car tipped on every turn. He'd leave it in the street and take the stairs three at a time. At home he would follow her from room to room, staying within a few feet of her body. Tonight he'd get into bed with her, and for a little while he wouldn't throw anything. Now she was just waiting, in her torn and muddy stockings, holding Hank, who had spent most of the afternoon crying.

"When?" Charlie wailed. He'd had no nap, none of them had had a nap, and everything was tragic to him now. He put his elbows on Marcelline's lap and gazed up at her, red-eyed, as if he'd known her all his life. She was telling him something about some seals that lived near the island. You could see them, she said, going home to sleep near the lighthouse, about sunset. Her little boys liked to go see them, and she'd take David and Charlie and Hank there, if it was all right with their momma, to see the seals going to bed, just as soon as they were finished here.

"Let's go *now*," Charlie said.

"Soon, darling," Marcelline crooned, patting his head. "Soon as those men let your momma go."

Finally the door opened, and a square-shaped blond man in a black navy uniform came in. Over one arm were her drapes, neatly folded. While the FBI men questioned her, one of them had slit the hems open with a pocketknife. Now they were folded to appear whole. He handed them to her with large square fingers, the nails so clean they looked like glass.

"You're free to go now, Mrs. Hooper." He glanced at Marcelline. "I understand Miss Johnson here has volunteered to give you a ride home. Or to the airport, if that's where you're going." He never quite met Ella's eyes. "If you want your buggy back, I'm afraid you'll have to call the Bridge Authority."

Ella watched him, waiting for him to go on. "But he's coming here?"

"I'm sorry, who?"

"My husband."

The officer focussed on her, blinking.

"Someone did talk to my husband? Did he not say he was coming here?"

"No. I don't believe he did say that."

"Did he give you any message for me?"

He smoothed down his cuffs. "There was a message, yes."

56

She waited, leaning forward.

"He said thanks — thanks for the ten dollars. That was it. Thanks for the ten dollars."

❖❖❖

"You still have plenty of time." Marcelline knew all about the night flight to New York — it was the one her fiancé took. "We'll just stop off for a minute and see the seals."

She drove onto Yerba Buena and took a dirt road out onto a high point jutting over the water. Her car was big, a big white American car with loose springs, and it wallowed through the ruts in the road, coming to rest in a stand of dark cypress.

They stood on the edge of a cliff, looking west under the bridge. The sun was red and round, low over the ocean, and they could see part of it through the Golden Gate. The bay shimmered pink and gray, with dark blue water behind them.

Marcelline pointed to the water. A confusion of waves washed back from the cliffs, glinting and rocking. "Keep your eyes right there. Right by those rocks. They'll be coming under the bridge any minute now, right at us. Keep your eyes open, now."

They stood and stared for a long time. The air was cold, and they started to shiver. The boys pressed against Ella's body for warmth.

57

"There they are!" Charlie shrieked. He clutched her legs.

They all stared hard. Suddenly over the water was a row of black stitches, then only water. Tiny black arches — water. Black torpedoes — gone underwater. Up they flew, looped under, leapt again. Brown sea lions, sleek with water, flippers back, flying through air, so close under the cliff you could almost see the gleam in their black eyes.

Charlie's hand gripped her knee, fingernails biting her skin through the holes in her stocking. His voice was high and thin. "Why don't they stay under the water? Why don't they stay under the water where they belong?"

David lifted his hands like claws. He opened his mouth, menacing Charlie with small spaced teeth. "Shark. Shark chases them."

Ella put her arms around Charlie. "No. That is not the reason."

He looked up at her fearfully. "What is it?"

"Joy," she said.

AFFECTION

❖·❖·❖

─────────────── AS A BABY, MY FATHER
claimed, I was a cat. I don't know what hard evidence
he had, but at one time I played along with him to
the extent that, when introduced to strangers, I fell
on all fours (I'm not proud of this) and said meow.
Later I acquired every known cat toy: stuffed cats,
china cats, cat books and posters, a cat pin, cat eras-
ers, a cat lunchbox and toothbrush, a blue felt circle
skirt with appliquéd cats, and sheets with kittens
printed out of all spatial sense. I also lobbied without
cease for an actual cat, wearing my mother down
until she suddenly agreed, apparently out of mere
exhaustion, the year my third older brother joined
the others in their loud and hungry teens.

Seymour spent his kittenhood in my room. My
brothers were forbidden to approach my door, and I
tried to stand guard around the clock, until my parents made clear that I would still have to go to school.

When the bell rang in the afternoon, I was on my bike before most kids cleared their seats, racing home in panic, trying to beat my brothers. Soaked and panting, I didn't slow down until I made it to my door. But then I stopped, opened it a quarter inch at a time, in case he was behind it.

Sometimes he was hard to find in that wilderness of false cats. He'd be caught halfway up a curtain, big-eyed, mewing for help, or curled in a perfect circle on the bed, surrounded by the rubble of his day, torn magazines and lamps overturned on their shades. Impossibly small and light, at first he was no more than the idea of a cat, a loud purr in electrified fur, a dandelion with claws. Ten times a night I'd wake up afraid of crushing him, feel for him on the bed, and he'd start to purr. Once after dinner he was gone. I panicked, accused my brothers, forced a search of their rooms. Hours later, exhausted from weeping, I opened my bottom drawer and found him curled peacefully on a sweater.

When my brothers were not at home, I introduced him to the backyard. Staggering across the lawn, he recoiled at grass blades, arched his back and hissed, or charged suddenly at nothing, scaring himself. For a long time he was relieved to go back to my room, purred loudly when he found the soft warm bed.

Then one day I saw him leap to the top of my

bookshelf from a standing start. When he jumped off the bed, you could hear the thud from anywhere in the house. He sat for hours on the windowsill, lashing his tail as he stared outside, or into the closet with his ears perked, listening for mice. He was a big gray cat with a white belly and paws, like a fish designed to blend both with dark water, when seen from above, and light sky, when seen from below. The two-tone scheme extended to his nose-tip and paw-pads, which were half black, half pink. In his green eyes the black could be round and shiny as an eight ball, tight as a stitch, or like a watermelon seed. When I opened the door of my room, he loped across the floor, making a break for the outside.

"Yaaaaaaaaaaaaaaaaaaaaa," my brother Charlie said, eyes crossed, tongue flapping while he jerked his body like Frankenstein, the first time he met Seymour on the lawn. Dropping to a crouch, Seymour eyed him, and fled sideways, out of the yard.

❖❖❖

"What's a cat's favorite drink?" my father said and took the library card out of my book. Removing the pencil stub from behind his ear, he started doodling on it.

I didn't bother to answer. I was only out there on the deck, sitting in smoke and fumes from the barbecue, because inside Hank was torturing his saxophone, and a cat's favorite drink was a very old joke. If I gave the obligatory response (mice tea) there would be no stopping him. What do cats put in their lemonade, he'd want to know. What's their favorite dessert, their favorite weather, their favorite exercise. Where do they take their children on Saturday afternoons.

Solemnly he slid the card back into the pocket at the back of my book. Paying no attention, I secretly worked it out of the pocket to where I could see it. Drawn on the card was a ladybug meeting a Sugar Smack. They were the same shape, ovals, with spots. The ladybug had legs, the Sugar Smack didn't, but the resemblance was close enough. The ladybug gazed at the Sugar Smack, and a heart rose from it. The caption read "Love Stinks."

"So," my father said. "How's your cat?"

"Fine." As far as I knew, that was the case: he stopped by every day to eat, usually in the early morning before the boys were up. He no longer came home at night, and I had no idea where he was spending his time, but he seemed fine.

A boy called out from the backyard, and David's hightops squeaked across the kitchen floor.

"You weenie!" he howled, banged open the sliding screen and pounded down the steps to the yard.

"David!" my mother yelled from inside.

David dashed up the steps, giggling, ran into the

kitchen, slammed the glass door and locked it behind him. Charlie ran up panting, put his hands on either side of the door and lifted it off its runner. He propped it against the wall and plunged inside.

Shouts, cries, pounding feet on stairs. "Did not," we heard, and "don't you ever." Doors slammed upstairs.

"I thought I saw him the other day," my father said, starting a doodle on a paper napkin. "Across the street. At the new people's house." He paused thoughtfully. "I could be wrong, but it looked as if he was pawing their front door."

"Oh, sure," I said. By no outward sign did I reveal that I had been shot through the chest with a hot dart. "He gets around. Cats have resources, you know — they're not like dogs. They make their own friends. It's an honor when they come around."

He raised his eyebrows without looking up from his drawing. "An honor. Yes, that's certainly true."

Inside, voices started again, my mother's and Charlie's. The front door banged open, and Charlie ran by in the driveway above us, headed for the garage. My mother was close behind him, his motorcycle helmet dangling by its strap from one hand, her arm straight down at her side. He pushed his motorscooter up the driveway to the street. She followed with quick graceful steps, shoulders back, head up, like a diver approaching the end of the board. He reached the sidewalk, paused to throw one leg over the bike. She swung the helmet over her head, straight-armed, slammed it into the concrete. It bounced with a sharp crack.

"That is what's going to happen to you, young man!" she said.

Charlie buzzed away without looking back. My mother walked quickly back to the house, head up, shoulders back. The helmet rolled over twice and stopped, teetering in the driveway. My father rose and went to pick it up.

◆◆◆

The new people's house was just across the street, but it was hard to see from where I was. Like most of Berkeley, our street was on a steep hill. We lived on the downhill side, hanging out into air, and the top of our house was only about as high as the sidewalk on the other side. To see anything I had to cross the street, climb up into their yard.

Their red convertible was in the driveway, and most of the windows in the house were open, with curtains blowing out. I didn't have a plan. With anyone else I could have gone over to play with the kids, but the new people didn't have any, not even a dog or a cat. I considered them the most uninteresting family I had ever seen.

At the top of their driveway was a gate, but when I got to it I heard voices in back. Veering away, I crossed the front yard, searching the shrubbery as if for a lost ball. On the other side of the house was a new redwood fence, still smooth and faintly red, not gray and prickling with splinters like ours. Standing on a large ornamental rock, I could see over the top.

The last people that lived here had kids, and in those days the backyard was a dead lawn/dog bathroom, equipped with hula hoops, pogo sticks, mole mounds and a tetherball pole in a bare circle. Now suddenly it looked like a picture in a magazine: a new deck, a tall hedge, massed flowers in orderly bloom.

The hedge blocked my view of the lawn, but through it I thought I saw a flash of gray and white. My heart started to pound. I hauled myself to the top of the fence, trying to see better, then dropped to the ground on the other side. I didn't care — let them catch me. I had to find out.

One corner of the deck met the house not far from where I landed. Maybe I could make it, maybe not. The deck was only about four feet off the ground, with azalea bushes planted around the edge. Getting through the azaleas without rustling would be tricky, and when I got there, I tried not to touch them at all.

The people were on the other side of the deck, talking and laughing loudly, and they didn't seem to notice me. Underneath, there was a hint of musty catbox, but the old dead grass was still in place, so I didn't have to crawl in the dirt. From there, I could see the whole yard.

It was Seymour all right. Across the soft new lawn, in the shade of the hedge, he lay on his side like a lion, looking up, exposing his white underchin and belly fur. His head tracked a bug, he snapped at it, missed. Lowering his chin, he surveyed the yard.

I lifted my head above the azaleas, and he gave me a long intense look. Blinking, he turned away, licked his shoulder with sudden energy.

"So there we were, still in the cab, for God's sake —," a man's voice said, up on the deck. A woman gave a high quick laugh, and another man said "Oliver" in a warning tone.

I could see slices of them through the slats — it was the new people and another man. The new people were both tall and blond, the woman in a white sundress and the man in seersucker pants. The other man, the one named Oliver, was dark and had on white trousers. Through the slats, they all moved in flickers, like an old movie, up there in the yellow light.

"No, you have to believe me, I swear it," the man named Oliver said, and the new people laughed uneasily.

"If it's anything like the last one —," the man who lived there said.

"No, no, it isn't, believe me. So there we were, we'd hardly said eleven words to each other, and there we were —" He went on to describe several forms of torture I'd heard about on the playground, emphasizing how much the woman in the taxi wanted him to do those things to her. The new people's laughter got higher and thinner, with gaspy pauses, until his voice ran down. Nobody said anything for about a minute.

"Oh, kiss and tell, Oliver," the woman said.

Both men laughed quickly, as if surprised. She stood up, walked across the deck and down the steps to the lawn.

My heart was thudding so hard I could see it in my eyes as I shrank down behind the azaleas. Chin pressed to the dirt, I watched her cross the grass. Her dress was printed with red roses, her blond hair in a ponytail down her bare back.

I couldn't see her face, but I knew she was pretty, because I'd seen her once close up. I was passing their house on the sidewalk when she came running down the driveway, chasing the blond man, who was trying to get away from her, striding toward the red convertible, parked at the curb. She was inches behind him, half laughing the way you do when you're playing a joke on someone, or chasing them and about to make the tackle. She had on jeans, a man's shirt and loafers, hair pinned to the back of her head, while the man was wearing a suit and tie.

"Just tell me who she is," the woman said. "Just tell me how you met her!"

"No," the man said, opening the door of the convertible.

"Just tell me how you met her! Is she one of your patients? No, you have to —"

The man shrugged her off, closed the door, but she reached in and grabbed the shoulder of his jacket.

"Just tell me how you met her!" She was yelling but still keeping her voice down, quieter than it would have been, and half laughing.

The man started to drive, the woman running along beside him, still gripping his jacket. As they passed me, he looked right at me and blushed. I was surprised to see that close up his face wasn't handsome at all, almost ugly as he grimaced at me. He drove off, breaking her hold on his jacket. She turned quickly, without glancing at me, and went into the house. I hadn't seen them again until now.

Seymour came out from under the hedge as she approached it and gave a pitiful meow, opening his pink mouth wide as a baby bird's. She stooped to pet his head, and he flopped onto his side, offering her the soft white fur of his belly. She stroked from his throat all down his underside, and he stretched his front legs forward and his back legs back, arching his neck. The tip of his tail started curling and uncurling. In a minute he would take hold of her wrist with his claws and teeth, play-biting, getting harder if she didn't stop.

When he grabbed for her, she laughed and scooped him up. She held him just right, his back supported on her arm, as she walked over to a bench under a low tree. She sat down, stroking his whole body, and he sprawled across her lap, kneading her with his paws. Taking a bit of dress between his teeth, he closed his eyes and kneaded her intently, a spot of cat drool spreading on her dress.

"Look at that, Oliver," the man who lived there said. "Isn't that an inspiring sight? Woman and child — it doesn't get better than that. You're looking at the goddamn inspiration of all great art. Don't you think it's an inspiring sight?"

"Woman and child," Oliver said, and ice clicked against glass.

❖❖❖

I expected to be caught every second, but they walked right over me to dinner without seeming to notice. The next afternoon, no cars were in their drive, and I went over again, to see if he was still there. Nobody asked where I was going. These days, my mother said "What!" if I went near her, and once I saw her sitting with her elbows on the kitchen table and her hands over her eyes. She considered "playing" enough of an answer for where I'd been.

Seymour was there all right, making free with the house and grounds. I stayed back near the fence, where he wouldn't have to notice me, and he didn't seem to mind. He dozed on the deck, rolled in the flower beds, strolled along the top of the high fence. From an oak tree he leapt to an open window on the second floor. With one quick ripple of his back, he slipped under the sash, calling out a meow. After a while he came out, sat on the sill in the sunshine and licked his paws. Jumping to the tree, he shinnied backwards down the trunk. Pausing at the bottom, he blinked, stalked toward the hedge.

Hunched in the shadow, he waited, looking up. The hedge was in bloom, studded with red flowers, and a hummingbird hovered along it, sticking its needle-nose in every one. Flat along the ground, Seymour crept up fast and launched himself into the air, all twenty claws aimed for the bird. The hummer darted just out of reach, chittering angrily, while Seymour crashed down through the hedge, holding his position as if frozen, claws clutching air, and landed in a heap. Standing up, he shook himself and stalked away, thrusting his shoulders forward like a panther.

A car door slammed in the driveway. Seymour crouched under the hedge, and I made it under the deck one heartbeat before she came through the gate with bags of groceries.

Walking back and forth to the car, she paid no attention to Seymour. The third time she passed him with her arms full, he charged out, grabbed her calf with his paws, eyes black and round as if he had scared himself. She laughed, and he darted back under the hedge, drawing himself up fearfully. But when she went by again, out he charged, gave her a two-pawed bat and dashed back in. She crouched down, tried to tickle his chest.

"Am I dead yet?" she said. "Did you get me yet?"

He pulled back, staring at her hand as if she had a knife in it. Suddenly he pounced, grabbed her wrist, pawed her hand with his back feet and leapt back under the hedge. He pounced, pawed, retreated, pounced, until she got tired of him.

❖❖❖

She didn't let on that she saw me that day, but I was sure somehow she knew. When I saw her in the street, I rode away furiously on my bike or went wild and yelled something stupid at the nearest kid. Even so, I couldn't stop. Whenever she drove away, I had to sneak up, climb the fence, snoop around their yard, whether he was there or not. If I tried to do something else, I had eyes in the back of my head, pointed at their house, until I forgot everything and raced toward it.

One evening, late that summer, I was near the front door when someone rang the bell. I opened it, not thinking much about it. My heart nearly stopped. It was the woman, and she had Seymour in her arms.

Someone grabbed my shoulders from behind. "Don't you ever open the door at night," my mother said and yanked me back into the hall.

I sat on the bottom stair, where I could watch through the banister. From the living room came boys' voices yelling, "Come on! Come on!" and a distant crowd-roar.

"I'm sorry to bother you," the woman said hurriedly, adding her name and where she lived. She was dressed up, in high heels and a linen suit, her hair in a French roll.

"Yes, and you have our Seymour." My mother did not say her own name in return, and she reached for him, pulled him away from the woman before she started to hand him over. The woman looked startled and put her arms out, one second after it was no longer necessary to do so.

"Someone told us he might be your cat," she said in a flat, even voice, as if she was reading it.

"And we were wondering — he seems to have some sort of abscess, on his paw —"

I stood up, tried to see around my mother's arm. She took hold of one paw, and he tensed, flipped over, climbed her shoulder. Behind us, my father came up to watch.

"The left rear," the woman said quietly. "We didn't like to take him to the vet without —"

"Thank you very much," my mother said and turned away. She started to close the door.

My father caught it over her head, and she ducked under his arm, carried Seymour to the kitchen. My father stepped into the doorway. He was so tall he had to stoop slightly to get under the frame. "So. Let's see. What shall we call it? Catnapping?"

The woman looked up at him and blushed. "We didn't exactly — I'm sorry, but you see, we didn't think he had a home." She examined my father. "He seemed to be throwing himself on our mercy."

"We thought someone must be keeping him in."

She gasped slightly. "You make it sound like we use little chains and handcuffs. It isn't exactly like that — he begs to come in. We've tried ignoring him, but he wakes us up at night, and he won't take no for an answer. Once he pawed our door for an hour and a half." She held up her hands, palms out, and paddled the air, as if begging to come into our house. "We thought he was hurting his paws."

My father took a step out onto the stoop, lowering his voice. "Alienation of affection, then. You've heard of that? You can sue the corespondent for it, in a divorce."

The woman smiled slightly, looking up at him. "Without of course being at fault oneself."

My father stepped all the way out, pulled the door closed behind him.

"Jesus, don't they know how to get rid of a cat?" Charlie said, laughing, in the kitchen. "There's nothing to it. You just go yaaaaaaaaaaaaaaaaaaaaaa."

In a flurry of white paws, Seymour shot around the corner. Casting me a black-eyed look, he put his nose to the bottom corner of the front door, batting with a soft paw.

"In a minute," I whispered, picking him up. "You can go back out in a minute. If you go right now they'll catch you, because they're both still out there."

I carried him up the stairs, and he watched nervously over my shoulder. At the window on the landing I showed him: my father and the woman were standing on the sidewalk in the fading light, blocking escape by the front door.

❖❖❖

"Cat patrol," my father said a couple of weeks later, throwing down his napkin after dinner. "I'll just go get him, so Jane can have him for a while before she goes to bed."

I followed him out into the hall. "That's all right, Dad. Don't worry about it."

Seymour had been jailed in my room the whole time he was on antibiotics, on orders from the vet. He spent it sitting on the windowsill, lashing his tail, or meowing at the door to get out.

"It's okay. I'll see him in the morning, when he comes over for breakfast."

"He's your cat."

"I know. But don't worry about it."

He put his hand on the doorknob. "You stay here. I'll be right back."

An hour later he brought Seymour up to my room and shut him in. Heading straight for the closet, he sat in the dark, wide awake, eyes reflecting light when I opened the door to see how he was. I waited until the house settled down for the night, then let him out by the front door.

Soon we had the routine down: carried back after dinner, he went to sleep in my bed, until some dark and silent hour. Sleep was something he understood, and he woke me up as gently as it can be done: nose close to my face, he purred, or gave a soft chirp. Together we padded down the stairs in the dark, his fur brushing my leg under the gown. I only had to open the door a few inches, and in the fainter dark outside I watched him snake around it. Trotting away up the walk, his ears were alert, fur fluffed with excitement.

"But he comes back every night," the woman said, laughing on our front stoop with my father. It was the first rain of the year, and he and I were out there watching it when she drove up. She waved to him as she got out and called something I couldn't hear, then came across the street, smiling in a tan raincoat. Her hair was getting wet, and my father told her to come up under the eaves.

She smoothed her wet hair back out of her face. "He comes in the window about three o'clock in the morning and jumps on the bed, cheerful as can be. So glad to see us, and would we mind getting up and fixing him a snack? If we close the window, he sits in the tree and yowls, about five feet from our ears. That's a sound that could go through concrete. Cat from Mars, Sam calls him."

My father turned elaborately to look at me, but I was backing through the doorway, into the hall, out of reach.

Down in the darkroom my mother called his name. Soon she came up the stairs, two at a time. Headed for the study, she noticed the open front door and stood still, watching.

"Maybe if he had a way to get back in here at

night," the woman said. "Maybe he comes here first, and can't —"

"A cat door," my father said. "We thought of that. But — the raccoons. Have you got raccoons? We've got raccoons, and skunks, and once in a while even —"

My mother stepped out the door. "You have to go get Hank this minute." She took hold of his arm, tried to pull him into the house.

"Okay," my father said, and she let go, stepped inside.

"But if he tries to come in here at night, and he doesn't have a way —," the woman said.

My mother stepped out, took hold of him again. "Right now. You can do this later." She was much smaller than my father but pulling so hard he had to step inside. She closed the door behind him.

"Jesus, Ella," he said.

She yanked his raincoat out of the closet and shoved it at him. "You said you were going twenty minutes ago! What does it take!"

From the window on the landing I watched the woman cross the street, flipping her collar up. When she reached their driveway, Seymour dashed out from under a bush and loped ahead of her with long easy strides. He got to their front door first.

My father ran across the street, holding his

raincoat. He caught her arm just before she opened her door. Seymour pressed up against it, arching his wet back, meowing at them until they went inside.

❖❖❖

My father didn't say anything to me, but he stopped going over after dinner to bring him back. It wasn't long after that before Seymour stopped coming over for breakfast. I was the only one who noticed at first, and I had time to figure out what had happened before anyone else.

Across the street, the woman's car was gone, and the windows in the house stayed closed for days. The man drove up at night in the red convertible and away again in the morning, always alone. After he left, I'd walk right up their driveway, open the gate and sit on the deck. Along the hedge, hummingbirds sipped the lowest flowers undisturbed.

Once I went over after a hard rain. Fat white clouds were sailing away over the hill, leaving the sky empty and blue. Steam rose from their deck, shining in the sun. I lay down on the boards and rested my nose in a crack. The wood was warm and smelled of sweet spice, with gusts of catbox underneath. I thought about Seymour as a kitten, how he slept on my chest and mewed, heartbroken, if I put him down. Later he was so tender with my sleep.

Maybe I should have known. One summer

78

morning as I walked by, pretending not to stare at the new people's house, I noticed something on their front stoop. Their curtains were still closed, and I went up quickly to see what it was.

Side by side on the doormat lay two dead mice. They were perfectly lined up, with each other and the door, stiff tails pointing the same direction. One's head was thrown back in agony, exposing a triangle of tiny teeth. The other lay on its side, glassy black eye open, paws curled. Both gray coats were matted with cat spit, but they were almost unmarked, a tiny drop of clotted blood on one, and nothing eaten.

Gardeners policed the new people's yard, packed redwood chips around authorized plants and left no leafy corners along the fence. The lower slopes of our yard, on the other hand, were a tangle of blackberry vines, nasturtiums and bindweed, home to salamanders, mice and even snakes. After catching the first mouse, Seymour must have carried it in his mouth while he climbed the steps to our deck, passed our kitchen door, climbed our driveway, passed our front door, crossed the street, climbed their steep yard and placed it carefully on their doorstep. Then he had to go back down and do it all again.

I imagined Seymour on a beach. The woman held him on her lap, both of them in sunglasses. A cool drink was on the table and a bowl of catfood underneath. By now she must know what kind he liked: land animals were only worth a sniff, the dried stuff not even that. Most fish he would eat, though for some kinds he stayed on his feet, drawn up away from the bowl. Only for tuna would he sit all the way down.

Maybe there would be fishing boats pulled up to that beach. Maybe Seymour would meet them, leap aboard, rub the fishermen's legs. Maybe the boats caught tuna. Maybe Seymour stowed away on a tuna boat, lived with the fishermen, left that woman on the beach.

❖❖❖

One night my father did not come home for dinner. My mother didn't say anything about it, and she didn't yell at Charlie or say much of anything else. She waited dinner until we were all half starved, but none of us talked about it. We just lay around in the living room, playing games and pretending to read, and even the boys were quiet. It got to be seven, seven-thirty, quarter to eight.

"Come to the table," my mother said.

"Aw, let's wait for Dad," Charlie said, but she was spooning food onto plates.

She left his place set, pans covered on the stove, and sat in the kitchen, writing Christmas cards, near the wall phone. It rang twice, both for Charlie. It was almost ten before she remembered to send me to bed.

The house was dark and still, and I must have been asleep a long time when I suddenly woke up. I always slept with my door closed, but now it was open. A soft heavy object hit the floor. The door closed silently, the latch clicked and footsteps went down the stairs.

In the faint light from the window, I saw a shape like a shepherd's crook go by the bottom of my bed. A moment later it came back, twitching slightly. I thought I heard purring. Suddenly the bed compressed, and heavy soft feet stepped on my shins. Even in the dark I could see his white mask. He was purring louder than I'd ever heard and kneading the bed at every step, claws catching in the comforter.

"No," I said. "You don't live here anymore."

The purr was deafening when he reached my face. He brought his nose close, touched my forehead, gave me one quick lick, as if to see who I was by taste.

"Forget it, Seymour. You made your choice."

Circling around by my chest, he kneaded the covers just right. He curled down against my side but kept his head up, ears pointed toward the door. Purring thrummed through the bed.

"Okay, look. It's late. But only for tonight. No promises. Understood?"

He didn't turn down that diesel purr one bit.

DEATH ANGEL

TONIGHT THERE ARE puppies, some sad mix, maybe dachshund and shepherd, left for David by the guy on days. They aren't going to be cute later, but now they are like all puppies, warm round bellies, soft tongues that lick your face, and the day guy couldn't face it. It was easier with the older dogs — street dogs, garbage-eaters. They smelled foul, were usually half sick, tried to hump your arm or bite when you opened the cage. David just looked them in the eye while he put the needle in, said, "Okay, buddy, this is it, you or me, you knew it would come to this." They got high on the way down and seemed to like it, lying back drooling, twitching one patchy leg.

He saved the puppies for last, did the other chores first. Whenever he went past their cage, they piled up at the bars, paws on each other's backs, chewed each other's ears, snarled little wet snarls. He stopped and held his knuckle to the bars, and one licked it. Reaching in, trying to get the right one in the mass of waving tails and licking tongues, he lifted it out and held it against his tee shirt.

"Yo, don't lick the death angel."

The puppy reached its nose up, pink tongue darting out, trying to lick his face. Death angel — funny he thought of that. It was a mushroom that grew in the hills in the wet season. Tiny, slender and white, even one could wipe out a whole dinner party. This winter they were getting a lot of rain, and over Christmas it had happened more than once, in Berkeley and other places around the bay. Of course it might not always be an accident. Spend a couple of years tramping around in muddy boots, scrambling up ravines and forcing harmless mushrooms on your friends, then one gloomy Christmas Eve you slip one of the little white ones in with the brown and take along your wife, your mother-in-law, the chairman of your department, whoever you have in mind, and nobody calls it murder and suicide.

The puppy wiggled around, whined little calls to its brothers in the cage, waved its floppy tail. David took the others out, one at a time, petted and played with them, so he'd know exactly what he was doing later. He wasn't trying to torture himself — he just wanted to see things the way they were. The shelter was in the flats along the bay, on landfill made from garbage, and people from the hills didn't want to know what went on down there. They didn't want to see those plastic bottles after they threw them out, or know what happened to the wino in the park after they called the cops. They might call the dogcatcher to pick up a stray, but they didn't want to hear about what happened after. David was from the hills too, and he knew he wasn't doing anything different, except looking. But on the way to work he let the bike roll slowly, took note of the junkies, the winos, the bag ladies, the whores, the chemical dumps.

When he finished the chores, he took the puppies out one at a time. They whimpered when they felt the needle, chewed his hand, fell asleep against his chest.

"This is it, buddy," he told them, stroking their small bodies. "That's the only shot you'll ever have. You'll never get worms, or spend the day tied up barking off your head. You won't have to eat dry food, or get kicked in the mouth by a guy on a loud bike. No one's going to cut off your nuts, and you won't get fleas or cancer. You won't even know that you were only a dog and not the king of the universe. You're the king of the universe, buddy," he said.

❖❖❖

Around midnight, he took the steep streets past dark houses at close to sixty, or at least fifty-five, so the bike slit the belly of the quiet, engine noise spooling out behind. Tonight the fog was in, lashing in front of his lights, sealing him into a fast-moving pocket of sound in the silvery quiet, and wetting his long hair. He never wore a helmet, not just for the feel of the wind. A guy he'd known all his life, whose dad taught in his dad's department, had turned his brain to butterfat with an easy fall, while wearing a helmet. He was only doing about twenty-five when a car backed out of a driveway in front of him. He slid out, landed on his chin, drove the jawbones up into his skull. What was the point?

His parents lived near the top of the Berkeley ridge, and the fog was thick up there, down to the ground, dripping off trees. He purred quietly up their block, cut the engine and rolled down the drive, casing the house. He could hardly see it, but he thought there were no lights on this side. By now his mother and little sister would be asleep, and his younger brother would have sneaked out to go climb in some girl's window. Only his father would be up, in his study, around on the downhill side of the house.

He went quietly down the steps to the deck off the kitchen. On clear nights you could see San Francisco, the bay, the bridges, Oakland, the works, and on nights like this a thousand streetlights tinted the fog a faint radioactive orange. It seethed around him as he leaned on a redwood bench, stretched his legs out, and rolled a slightly soggy joint.

He was about to light it when it occurred to him that tonight might be the time to turn on his old man, who had expressed an interest. David wasn't sure he wanted to, but he slid the joint into the chest pocket of his black tee shirt, where it couldn't get bent, and crept down the steps to the yard. He didn't know exactly what he was going to do, and he would watch what he decided, as a sort of experiment on himself.

His father's light shone on a dripping apple tree about ten feet below the window. From the crotch of the tree, he could usually see the top of his father's head and smell cherry pipe smoke. His father never slept before dawn, and he spent the night reading. Sometimes he was reading what he ought to be, but not often. He went on binges, consuming thousands of pages on Japanese drum rituals or the social life of ants. Whatever it was — a student paper, a profile of Jackie Kennedy, a critique of phenomenology, the day's junk mail — he pencilled tiny comments, sometimes with illustrations, in the margins. In fact, any paper, anywhere in the house, might provoke a pencilled annotation. "When I consider how my light is spent" once turned up on a square of toilet paper, several sheets inside the roll, and the hope of finding furious exclamations, or at least little shovels drawn in the margins, used to help David get through assignments in his schoolbooks. When his older brother Charlie was at home, still trying to become the youngest human ever to get into Harvard, he posted an improving list on his bedroom mirror, advising himself to read a hundred pages a day, spend less time thinking about sex, and keep his fingers off his face in public. Soon it also said, in tiny pencilled print, "Abstain from beans" and "Tuba practice, 6 a.m."

David pulled himself gently into the tree, careful not to shake off a shower from the leaves. The window was open and paper rustled inside, but he could not see or smell anything of his father. He made a tube of his fist and held it to his lips. "Who-oo," he called. "Who-oo."

The rustling stopped, but there was no reply, though David was sure he had been heard. His father had always been alert, ready to grab the ankle of a small boy creeping up behind him to, say, hang a leaf on his ear. He was unbeatable at basketball or tennis, though he was no athlete and relied on cunning, or at chess, where he seemed to know all of your moves before you did, nodded slightly when you made them, and made his own at once, needing no time to think. He was tall, with arms like an ape, and alarmingly still, good at long stares, long pauses before answering, and barely perceptible movements. He didn't smile much, except when he was mad or ironic, but he was always ready to stalk, ambush, capture and trick, with a straight face. He knew where to strike and would do so when ready, silently and fast, without warning. He seemed able to hear conversations behind closed doors in other parts of the house and to know which son was climbing in which window in the small hours, and even why.

Failure to respond to an owl call under the window, David knew, could be the lure of a trap set to snap closed when he entered the house. Now that he was old enough to think about leaving home, their relations showed signs of becoming more sensible, but not consistently. The week before, for instance, someone had induced a nest of tent caterpillars to attach themselves to the seat of his motorcycle, and lately he had started receiving catalogues through the mail. Some of them advertised black lingerie with lewd lacy cutouts, while others sold elephant guns, giant gold-plated bullets and camouflage briefs. Of course he was also getting recruiting letters from the CIA, which were probably not his father's doing, and glossy army brochures urging him to "Become a Missile Launch Officer — Launching Pad to Your Future!" Other guys his age were getting mail from the army too. Lately the President had been on television, saying "In-do-chi-na," square jaw flexing as he tried to get the strange word past a Texas accent. But no one else he knew was also on the mailing list for Frederick's of Hollywood.

Stealth was easy in the wet grass, the ground springy after months of rain. Careful not to snag any branches, he crept across the orchard and pulled himself up the rail of the balcony outside the living room. The sliding glass door was already unlocked, left that way by Hank on his way out, but it would give an unmistakable low rumble if slid, so he lifted it off its tracks instead and leaned it against the balcony wall. He eased his creaking leather jacket off his shoulders and down to the living room floor, and pulled off his boots and socks.

In uttermost Daniel Boone quiet he stole across the dark living room, feeling his way by the position of carpets, couches, tables, and patches of hardwood floor. He reached the bottom of the stairs and turned down the short hallway to his parents' bedroom and his father's study.

He listened at the door of the study. The desk chair gave an unguarded creak. Like a hawk stooping on the doorknob, he gave it a violent twist, meaning to fling it open and spring into the room in eerie silence, so as not to wake up his mother.

The knob gave a small, frustrated grunt, but refused to turn. The door was locked. Behind it, sudden furious movements, papers shoved aside, desk chair slightly rolled, then held-breath quiet.

He considered stealing away, as the spookier alternative, but he was curious about the new tactic of locking the door. He also felt a certain obligation to continue falling into the trap, having been snared this far. He considered his options. The study had another door, to the bathroom that connected it to his parents' bedroom. Getting into the bathroom, however, would involve entering the bedroom and possibly waking his mother up. She was a deep sleeper and could ordinarily be counted on to remain unconscious for the same seven hours every night, but she was also a person with strong opinions, who liked to think she was in charge of what went on around her house, even in the middle of the night.

What would happen if he woke her up? You never knew how she would react. Years ago, when he broke her rules (drinking from the milk carton, riding with no hands) sometimes she pretended not to notice, bored with police work. But then there were the other times. Once she made him take his clothes off on the playground of Hillside School. He was only about six or seven, young enough that she wouldn't let him walk home alone, and when she came to get him he was running and sliding with the other boys in a small lake left on the grass by a heavy rain. In a fury she ordered him to undress. When he wouldn't, she undid his muddy shirt and pants and pulled them off herself with trembling hands. He stood naked and crying on the grass while she walked away with his clothes. He ran after her and begged her to give them back, dancing on his bare feet and trying to cover himself with his hands, trying to hide both sides of himself at once.

Cautiously he opened his parents' bedroom door. The bed was on the far side of the room, set back in an ell, and it seemed possible to make the bathroom without waking her. When he glanced at it across the dark room, the bed looked surprisingly smooth, almost as if no one was in it. But that was typical of his mother, who believed that beds should be made up tight, and lain in straight.

He made the short passage to the bathroom easily. Inside, he closed the door but did not latch it, so it made no noise.

Light spilled under the door from the study. Carefully he knelt down and flattened his cheek to the cold tile floor, but all he could see was polished hardwood, gleaming yellow in the lamplight. Cool air blew through the crack, stinging his unblinking eyes.

He stood up and prepared himself. This door

was plainly going to be unlocked, and for the symmetry of it he threw himself against it, flung it open and leapt into the study exactly as he had intended to do before.

Leaning back in the desk chair, facing the bathroom door, arms and legs draped in a tense and awkward imitation of relaxation, was his mother. She was naked. She was not smiling. Her body was compact, athletic, slightly ravaged. Clinging to it here and there were raw fillets of ocean-going whitefish. Luminous, translucent white, they shone like oversized maggots on her freckled, brown and white, wrinkled, goose-fleshed skin.

❖❖❖

In the movies they print the leap twice, reversing it the second time, so the young man springs through the door, sees that the room is crawling with pit vipers, or two men who are trying to kill him, or his mother naked except for fish, and instantly he leaps back out, closing the door behind him. In life it is not so easy to leap backwards, through a doorway, between a toilet and a sink, land barefoot on a tiled floor, and close the door, too. His anklebone struck the toilet with a shuddering clang, and pain shot through it like a hot needle. For a moment, his whole leg went numb.

He limped through the bedroom, hallway, living room, out the balcony door, over the railing, and dropped to his good foot on the grass. He slumped to one side and lay quietly, holding his ankle. Waterdrops distilled from fog ran to the tips of leaves and plunked into moist earth.

He wasn't thinking yet, his mind stalled in the act of willing his eyes to go blank. Then it occurred to him, in a detached sort of way, that it was strange to have known her all his life and not to have known that she had orange pubic hair. The hair on her head was a thin yellow, lighter every year as more hairs came in white. But he had never bothered to wonder what color . . . As far as he was concerned, in fact, that part of her did not exist. Which was odd, considering that it had everything to do with him. He himself had at one time . . . If his eyes were open, it may even have been the first thing he ever . . .

Crouching, he ran lopsidedly across the orchard and up the steps to his bike. Luckily the keys were in his pants and not his jacket. He pushed the bike up the drive and freewheeled two blocks before starting it up.

Turning south, he traversed the ridge, headed for Marin Street. Originally laid out as a trolley line, it cut straight down the ridge, dropping a thousand feet in ten blocks. At each cross-street it momentarily flattened, then dropped again. In a car all you saw at first was hood, and on the bike his spine compressed at each flat spot. Then he left the ground, released higher and lighter every second until the bike paused, arced down until the rear tire brushed the falling road, teetering while the front wheel floated down, feeling for the bottom. Seconds later, faster each time, he hit the flat, the crunch of gravity, then soared again into the air.

He shot out into Marin Circle and looped around twice, tilted over deep. He pulled over to the curb and shook out his hair, looking back up Marin. Two of the cross-streets were major roads, and some-day, when he flashed through one of the stop signs, there was going to be a car in his way. But not this time. His feet were freezing, shudders running down his back under the tee shirt, but he couldn't tell if they were cold or joy.

He had the keys to the shelter, but it was a long ride back and there was nothing left to do — he had cleaned all the cages, fed the dogs and cats whose time was not yet up, incinerated the puppies with a squashed skunk brought in by Animal Control. Besides, he felt oddly unwilling to go too far from home. He took off up Arlington and made a circle around it, working his way up to the top of the ridge and turning south on Grizzly Peak, toward Marin.

He sat at the top looking out over the bay — he didn't need to go down again. The fog had lifted to become a low ceiling of cloud, and miles away across black water San Francisco glimmered through air so clear he could see stoplights change from green to yellow to red. Sounds came suddenly crisp through the washed air — the high ping of an electronic fog horn, a motorcycle climbing with a scream like ripping cloth.

His ankle gave a hot throb, as if an artery was tied in a knot, and he started to feel faintly ridiculous. For the first time it occurred to him to wonder what was happening at his house. Something had happened there earlier in the evening, and where was his father now? Possibly his mother was in some kind of trouble and needed his help. Up to now he had been trying to rub out his own error, hoping that, if he disappeared for a while, his mother might be willing to pretend she hadn't seen him — that he hadn't seen her — and neither of them would have to explain.

Suddenly he remembered the joint. His right palm flew up to his left pect as if pledging allegiance. His pocket was empty.

He ran through all of his recent moves, concentrating hopefully on the most recent, on the motorcycle. The wind would have tended to push it back into his pocket, not lift it out. Reluctantly he remembered further back and came to the moment when he knelt in the dark on the bathroom floor and pressed his cheek to the tiles. He saw his pocket sag gently open and the joint flop out on the floor.

He took the fastest route home. His father's car was not in the garage, though his mother's was. Why hadn't he checked for that before? He was a jerk, that's why — like a little kid, assuming everything would always be the same. He limped quietly down the steps to the deck.

Every light in the house seemed to be on. Standing on the deck, he could see his mother in the kitchen, wearing khaki slacks, a white turtleneck, a green sweater, leather boots with short heels and a plaid wool scarf looped around her neck, her hair pinned on top of her head in a tight bun. She looked as if she was ready to go out and do errands in the dark.

Her first glance at him was of pure terror, pale eyes so shiny they looked wet, mouth hanging slack — but maybe she couldn't see him through the reflection in the glass door. By the time he slid it open and stepped in, her face had relaxed, tipped back, her handsome lips protruding in the tight teasing smile she used with all the men in the family. She was so small and light, when she crossed the kitchen to meet him her boots made only a whisper, as if she hardly touched the floor.

She put her hand on his bare arm and stood too

close to him. Her face turned up to his, and her frail knees danced, hovering in a slight back-and-forth motion just in front of him, as if she wanted to move closer but wasn't sure of her welcome. She had always done that, and usually it felt good, like a cat rubbing his legs. This was the first time he had ever wanted to brush her off, like something unidentified running down his neck.

"Come in, you are chilled. Have you been out riding without even shoes? You know you could be hurt badly. Your arm is like ice."

Her voice rose and fell, inflecting English as if it were German, which always made him impatient. She'd only been in this country about twenty-five years, and she corrected them all when they said "Yeah" or "goin'" instead of "Yesssss" and "goinggggg." Why couldn't she hear the way English sounded? It wasn't a singsong, it was flatter, and the pitch varied all over the place. He took a step to one side, trying to get around her.

"And would you tell me what you think you are doing, removing doors in this house? That is not . . ." She danced back from him slightly, poking the air with her finger, almost stroking his chest. "I am really quite angry with that, I can hardly tell you. I hope that was the first time you have done such a thing behind my back."

"I'm sorry, Mom. I won't do it again. I'll just

put it back." He took an awkward giant step around her, toward the hall. If she didn't follow him, he might be able to duck into their bathroom, just for a second, and pick it up.

She took hold of his arm again. "I have already fixed it, and tomorrow I will have someone come to change the door so that it cannot be removed again. Now I want you to tell me exactly what sort of a circus you and your brother have been making of this house in the nights. You may start by saying what has happened to your brother."

Trapped, he leaned against the stove and looked down at her curiously. Hank? She was worried about Hank? Now?

"I have no idea."

She kept a firm, warm hold on his arm. "Yes, you do. I am sure of it. Where is he? He went to bed at eleven, and now he is not in the house."

He told her Hank had probably just sneaked out with his friends, that kids did that sometimes, and it was no big deal.

"Charlie never did anything like that, I am sure of it. Charlie was never secretive or sneaky, I knew everything that Charlie did. Why is it that you and Hank are turning out like this?"

David knew of a couple hundred things Charlie had done that she probably didn't know about, but he kept quiet. It was starting to dawn on him that, not only had she not found the joint, she was not going to say anything about what had happened earlier. She seemed to want to erase it as much as he did. Suddenly he was so relieved he almost wanted to hug her. He felt generous toward her, ready, even — well, almost ready to listen to her side in whatever had happened between her and his old man. His dad shouldn't leave her alone like this.

He let her talk about Hank and Charlie until she stopped on her own. He patted her shoulder. "I'm going to bed, Mom. It's late. You should, too."

"I want to talk to Hank. I will stay up until I see him. But you go to bed."

"All right. Can I do anything for you first?"

"No. Good night."

He started for the stairs, careful not to limp, but she followed him. She put her hand on his arm and gave him a dazzled look, pursing her lips — she seemed embarrassed, and was trying to cover up by pretending to feel playful. Two red spots formed on her cheeks, exactly where they are painted on the white face of a clown.

"You know, you children are not the only ones who play jokes with your father." She grinned up at him, unconvincingly, and shifted her weight back and forth, almost a prance. "You should not think too much about it." She gave a sort of chuckle.

"Sure," he said, and chuckled back. Stiffly, he patted her arm.

◆◇◆

He lay on top of the covers without taking off his clothes. The light from the kitchen came faintly up the stairs, and he was waiting for it to go out, and his mother to go to sleep, so he could get into her bathroom. The light was still on when he abruptly woke up. Downstairs, a glass door was rumbling open.

He couldn't make out the words, but he could hear his mother's voice rising and falling only slightly as she tried for a stern drone and Hank's deeper one competing with it playfully, teasing her, until she actually laughed. Hank was the only short male in the family, not much taller than she was, but he was wildly successful with girls and women. At seventeen, he had already been admitted through the bedroom windows of so many that he had strange ideas about most people's behavior. He once told David about a conversation with their father, in which Hank had supposedly asked him why he and their mother didn't start bringing lovers home. David couldn't imagine such words making it past his own throat while looking at his father, but he played along and asked what happened then. "Maintained the parental fictions," was all Hank said.

He was aware of voices diminishing downstairs. He fought to keep his eyes open, but the light was still on.

The next thing he knew, it was late morning. His ankle wouldn't straighten to go into the boot, so he put on a pair of old ripped tennis shoes and crept down the stairs. The house sounded empty. Ordinarily his mother would have been up since dawn, working in the garden or her darkroom in the basement, and by this time she would be out. But today there was no telling, after last night.

The door to the study stood open. He slipped into the bathroom and fell to his knees, patting the floor with both hands. He felt all over it a second time. It wasn't there.

Tracing his retreat through the house, he climbed over the balcony rail, dropped to the orchard. Thin sun shone on waterdrops in the grass. Kneeling in it, soaking his jeans, he parted the grass, but it wasn't there. It was not on the deck or in the driveway. He pushed the bike up to the street and rolled away, the engine catching with a roar at the bottom of the block.

◆◇◆◇◆

He stayed away from home all day, until time for work. That night, at the shelter, he finished the chores and sat around waiting for the doorbell to ring. People brought in animals at night, left them in the lockers out front and rang the bell. The lockers had two doors, a front one on the street and a back that could be opened inside the shelter lobby. When someone rang the bell, David was supposed to open the inside door and take out whatever they had left. Often the animals were dead, found by the road. But of course a person could put in anything they wanted, from a dead hamster to a live rattlesnake. It kept the job interesting in the quiet hours.

After a while the bell rang. He unsnapped the first few lockers, holding them closed until he knew what was inside. The ones he checked were empty, but before he had gotten to them all, the bell rang again.

He squinted through the one-way peephole in the door. Outside was a tall dark-haired white man with a huge face, the nose ballooning forward into his field of vision, the sides swept back toward the tiny distant street. He was looking down toward the sidepocket of his tweed jacket. Slowly he removed a pipe.

David opened the door. "Yo, Dad."

He gave David a nod, coming in. He studied the room, wall by wall, with a slightly puzzled look.

David waited, watching his face, secretly enjoying the ability to look straight across at it. Most of his life his father had been inscrutably tall, capable of unforeseen moves from above, but now they were the same size. They breathed a higher air than most, closer to the sky.

"So this is Doggie Dachau," his father finally said. "Show me around."

They looked at the holding pens, the office, death row. In the surgery, his father sat down beside the polished counter with the glass tray of needles. He started scraping out his pipe. David stayed on his feet, leaning against the counter, arms crossed on his chest.

"What'd you do to your foot."

He glanced down at it. "Nothing. Just a stupid accident."

"Not your bike, then. You wouldn't call that stupid."

David gave him a furtive smile, keeping hold of his lower lip with his teeth. His father watched him, and seemed to be waiting. After a while the lines of his face sagged slightly. He filled the pipe, lit it, and put the tools back in his pocket.

"It's an odd thing, but in some families, when the father disappears, even for a short time, the rest of the family — when he comes back — asks him a few questions."

David gave a short, unwilling laugh, and felt his cheeks burn. He felt suddenly angry.

"You really think our family is like anybody else's?"

His father raised his eyebrows. "I do. Yes, I definitely do."

David didn't want to say anything else, and he didn't think he was going to. Then he heard himself talking. "So. Let's see. Yes, I have a few questions. When did you take off? Was it before dinner? Were you supposed to be home for dinner, by any chance, and didn't make it?"

His father glanced at him, as if he was noticing something about him, but not as if he had been asked a question. David waited for an answer, but not long enough.

"I think she was planning to fix fish." He gave a foolish smile, and his heart started to thud.

"Fish," his father said. "Yes, I think that's a possibility." He studied David without saying anything.

For some time there was no sound except two dogs barking back and forth, down the hall in the holding pens. Casually David picked up a syringe. He examined it. When he got tired of waiting for his father to say something else, he put it down again, looked away and stretched.

His father took the pipe out of his mouth and waited for it to go out. "All right. Let me ask you something. Why did you take this job? Do you like killing dogs and cats?"

David didn't answer, just pressed his lips together and studied a point over his father's head. His father waited, and when it was obvious David wasn't going to say anything at all, his face softened slightly. He leaned forward on his knees, speaking quietly.

"I would have expected it of Charlie or Hank — there was a time when they both took animal life as a personal affront. Do you remember? From the time they were about two or three, they were stalking the neighbors' cats and getting mad as hell if a hummingbird had the nerve to come near our flowers. Anything moved, they wanted to kill it. The amount of bug death alone — if there's any justice, they'll both spend eternity staked to a red-ant mound, covered with honey." He leaned back, as if to see David better. "But they were safe with you. You wouldn't even let your mother take down spider webs in the garden. 'They live there,' you said. You were only about two and a half."

David folded his arms. He'd heard this one before. His father didn't repeat himself as much as some people's, and usually he told himself that it came from his dad's job: he had new students every year and it was okay to repeat himself to them, they'd never know it. They'd never realize they were getting that instead of something else.

"So you have trouble picturing me as the Butcher of Berkeley."

"Yes. *A little,*" his father said, with so much emphasis that it wasn't clear if he was being ironic. He might mean that it *was* only a little hard to picture David in that role, as if overt gentleness were just what it took to be able to slay kittens and puppies and forget it afterwards.

"I can help you with that. You can watch me do one. Would you like that? We have just one to do tonight." He took a step toward the door.

His father looked down toward the floor as if thinking about something else.

"If you don't want to, it's all right. I can do it later."

His father glanced up at him and nodded briskly. "No. I'd like to see it. Do it now."

David let out the skinny, shivering old dog. It shambled down to the end of the hall, toenails clicking on the concrete floor. They waited while it sniffed the hall and came cautiously into the room where they were, recoiling slightly from something it smelled.

"That's right, buddy, take a look around, see what's happening here," David said.

The dog limped toward them, lifted its nose and sniffed their hands without touching them. David filled the syringe and put it on the table. He caught the dog and lifted it gently, clasped under his arm.

"There, buddy. That's not so bad."

He rested its feet on the table and kept his arm over it while he reached for the syringe. The dog ducked its head and backed out of his grip. His father took hold of it just in time, before it could jump to the floor, and held it by the collar while David pushed the needle in.

"This is it, buddy," he said quickly, under his breath, so his father wouldn't hear.

The dog stopped quivering almost at once and just sat still. His father kept his hands on its head, absently massaging one ear. David stroked its back. Its coat was lumpy, grizzled with white and rubbed bare in places on the legs. Gradually the dog eased down, crossed its paws and put its muzzle on top. It sighed and closed its eyes.

They both kept stroking, careful to miss each other's hands. As the dog slumped over, they lengthened the strokes on down its legs. It took long quivering breaths, shorter and softer with each one, like incoming waves when the tide is going out. Finally they were so faint it was hard to tell when they stopped.

The dog lay flatter without the tension in its muscles. Its black lips hung slack, showing one white tooth.

His father crossed his arms and stood looking at

it. David put his ear to its chest, then stroked it a few more times.

"I like to wait till they cool off. It doesn't take long, and I like to make sure."

His father nodded vigorously. "Sure."

"You don't have to wait. It may take a while."

"What happens then?"

David told him about the incinerator. "That part can be sort of nasty, sometimes. And I won't do it for an hour or so — something else may come in. Something dead, I mean. You don't have to wait."

David followed him to the door. His father was all the way outside when he turned around.

"Oh. Almost forgot." He was holding the lighter to his pipe, and he gestured with his head. "Left something for you, in the locker on the end."

He stood there, lighting his pipe, and David felt his breath tighten down to a whistle, he didn't know why. They both nodded. His father walked across the street to his car.

He studied the door of the last locker. Of course he could leave it, and the day guy would find it in the morning, whatever it was, with the sad old raccoons and flattened cats brought in by the sheriff after he closed up.

Carefully he unsnapped the last locker. At first he thought it was empty, then he saw the small white cylinder lying on the bottom. The paper had come slightly unstuck, his spit having dried long since, and the dry flakes spilled out into his hand.

He carried it into the surgery, where the light was strong. His father's pencilled print was usually so small, he could have gotten on six lines of Shakespeare, a short biblical parable, or a limerick and a half. But this time the paper was blank and white. There was no message at all, that he could see, on the joint.

It was stupid to feel sad over nothing, and he wasn't going to. He got out his cigarette papers and rolled a new one tightly around it, licked it, pressed it closed and ran it through his lips to seal it tight. While the dog was burning, he propped the door open, sat outside on the curb. Usually he didn't smoke at work, but this time he thought, what the hell. Maybe he'd quit soon. Maybe it was time to get on the launching pad to his future. Carefully inhaling every wisp of smoke, he burned it all the way down, pinched it out, and ate the roach.

PUBLIC
HEALTH

◆◇◆

"AND WHAT ABOUT
for his other partner?" Dr. Burke said brightly, pen
hand over the prescription pad. She was gray-haired
and radiant, in flower-printed scrubs, and she gave
off an unnatural glow of serenity no matter what she
said. Over her desk, a pair of yin-yang fishes nuzzled,
nose to tail.

"His other —," I tried, and stopped. Partner
applied to dancing, and squash. It was slightly less
binding than buddy, as used at summer camp. "You
mean his wife?"

Dr. Burke smiled gently. "It won't work unless
we treat *all* of your partners, and all of your partners'
partners, at the same time."

I gave her a foolish grin. I couldn't get used to
having this sort of chat with the authorities. I was
much more at home in the infirmary at Radcliffe,
where the nurse used to draw the curtains around me,

turn her back and whisper, "I take it we're having a problem *down there?*" She praised me for knowing the use of a term like *genital,* since my knowledge must be largely theoretical. Here at Berkeley, only four years later, they assumed the students spent their evenings writhing, in groups, like frogs, and they tested you for gonorrhea if you came in with a sore throat.

"If we don't treat her, you see, she'll just keep giving it back to you, through him. But if you all three take the pills together, at the same time, you shouldn't have a recurrence. Unless of course —" She leaned on her fist, looking interested. "Unless of course *she* has other partners, as well."

She couldn't have known what she was saying — Edward's wife was from a different universe than Dr. Burke. Edward's wife committed her last error before she was toilet-trained, and she expected everyone else to do the same. She was German, a devout atheist, driven by obscure guilts. A former Olympic athlete, she spoke five languages, had produced four overachieving children, and she scrubbed the house down every day. In her spare time she strode around town in hiking boots, taking pictures that won prizes. She remembered Edward's every lapse in twenty-seven years of marriage, and she recited the list to him every now and then. She was also naive: "Ella assumes that everything is all right with us," he said, "so long as we fall into bed every now and then."

"No," I managed. "No, no."

"Are you sure?" Dr. Burke said calmly. "It's better to be certain, before we proceed. It's a good drug, but it shouldn't be overused. We have to be sure this time that *all* the partners —"

"But she doesn't have any symptoms," I blurted, unwillingly. It was appalling that I knew such a thing, about a woman I'd never met. I wasn't even anything like her: my achievements ran to numbers of cigarettes smoked, and a marriage that could have been measured in minutes. I had never been even adequate at any sport. My first-grade class had shared a mild case of polio, and I came out better than some of the rest — I only spent a few weeks in the iron lung, and I was out of leg braces inside of a year. But my feet never grew after that. They were tiny, stiff, too arched for flats. Unlike everyone else on the planet, I still wore heels, and walked with a mince I hoped looked vaguely French. I could never even have taken a walk with Edward's wife.

Dr. Burke nodded patiently. "Some women tolerate large numbers of these organisms, without symptoms, and therefore without needing treatment for themselves. But so long as she's part of *your* ecosystem —"

The last time, Dr. Burke had given me a prescription for three ("Eight tablets at bedtime, once only. #24"). I suppose she thought I'd call a meeting of the concerned parties and distribute appropriate medication. But Edward didn't even want to take it himself. You couldn't drink for days after, and he thought refusing wine with dinner would be a sort of scarlet letter on his shirt. As for giving it to his wife, what was he supposed to do, slip it in her orange juice?

"There has to be another solution," I said.

She shook her head, eyes bright, watching me. "There isn't one, I'm afraid."

I needed a smoke, and if I didn't get out of there fast, I was going to lose all dignity and weep. "All right, write it for three."

Dr. Burke started to write. Handing me the slip, she smiled into my eyes. "Why don't you let *him* worry about it, since it's his problem?"

❖◆❖

At Radcliffe I knew him as E. W. Hooper, the picture on the book jacket. My friend Ann and I were both in love with him — he looked boyish but tortured, exactly right for the intellectually pretentious young woman. Now there was a philosopher, we thought: why shouldn't they look like Byron, ready to ride all night in the rain for love, or tear out poor drowned Shelley's heart? One hardly ever met such people anymore. Imagine that scene on Long Island: Byron carries the body dripping from the Sound, helicopters hacking overhead, while a crowd gathers, dropping ice cream wrappers, shouting and shoving and chewing gum.

We chose Berkeley for graduate school because he was there, and we took all his classes. In person he didn't seem to have a light source in his eyes. But when he paced in front of the room, tall and lean, he moved like a baseball player, and sometimes when he was thinking he stared into my eyes across the room. He wrote a great deal on my papers (a fact I had to keep from Ann at first), and I suspected him of being freer in my margins than in anyone else's. "Learn from the jazz musicians," he advised, in tiny pencilled print. "If you make a mistake, don't take it back — repeat it." And: "The table seen from above and from below are two different tables; otherwise we'd look at 'Nude Descending a Staircase' and say 'Ah! Another picture of the Mona Lisa!'"

I hated weekends, the awful gap from Thursday to Tuesday when his class didn't meet, loathed summers and Christmas break, and dreaded the fulfillment of my course requirements. Apart from Edward, I had lost all interest in philosophy. I'd been interested in the subject since I was nine or ten and worried that, for instance, what other people called orange might look green to me, what I called green, and how could we ever know? — a question that still worries me.

But at Berkeley, in 1968, philosophy was being done with bullhorns, and that style was now adapted for classroom use. I wanted to castrate the men and pluck out the eyes of the women, a young professor had noted, in his evaluation of my first attempt at teaching. My only hope was to abase myself to my students, open my murdering imperialist heart, subvert the impulse to logical thought and let them copy their papers out of books. Did I want to become an instrument of surveillance? There was no healthy, positive alternative, but I might become a crack in the prisonhouse wall.

Thanks very much, I said, and starting thinking about some other line of work. But dropping out might not have helped — people I'd known all my life were starting to talk that way around the house. Ann now called herself a Maoist, as well as a Buddhist and a shiatzu masseuse. To further the aims of the universe, she had produced a child, and the two of us and the baby were living in a house with a pair of young men, naive Marxists I'd known since they were canvassing their elementary schools for Ike. Ann, Buzzy and Pete believed they were about to be arrested by the police, the FBI, the CIA, Billy Graham and Governor Reagan, working as a team, tipped off by the meter readers, the Avon lady and other representatives of the military-industrial complex, who'd give them shock treatment until they pledged allegiance to the flag. They went to meetings, passed out leaflets on the street, examined their consciences around the kitchen table. Evenings they would stun themselves with grass and lie motionless for hours in a room lit only by the red glow of the stereo, music so loud the room felt like the inside of a beating heart, remolding their DNA with lyrics like "I'm looking for someone to change my life. I'm looking for a miracle in my life." Daytimes they might give you a serene look and say, "The university you support developed the atomic bomb. Are you sure you want to be responsible for whatever they're making now?"

I don't know how exactly I got left behind, back in the region of complex distinctions. I supposed it might have something to do with drugs, which I did not take. I had nothing against the idea and was quite fond of Valium myself. But grass made me feel as if I was being watched, by someone like Sister Michael, my second-grade teacher, who thought that good girls didn't get sick, and therefore God had certainly made clear that there was something wrong with me.

"Why don't you at least try acid?" Ann sometimes suggested gently. "Find out what it's all about?"

I didn't care for paisley, I said, particularly not on the insides of my eyelids. If I *wanted* to see snakes ooze from walls, that would be one thing. According to Timothy Leary, acid gave the microphone of consciousness to cells in your spinal cord that had never heard of you, and was that supposed to be a *recommendation?* One of my housemates' favorite trips started with eating cactus buds and throwing up. Once they dropped acid before a party, and they didn't come down for a week. Somebody put some in the punch, and half the party ended up on Mars.

I went on listening to Mozart and trying to read philosophy. I made Edward my director and prepared to write my dissertation with him. ("Under" him, most graduate students said, "I'm working under so-and-so," and I blushed every time I heard it.) At night I dreamed about him, repetitious fables in which he loved me, kissed me, took me to bed. Awake, I accused myself of every known cliché. My desire for Edward was not love but an unresolved Electra complex, or a disguised class aspiration, or a rejection of my gender. I wanted to be singled out, raised above my station, like Cinderella, picked by the prince, or the Virgin Mary, alone of all her sex, the way some men yearn to be Robin Hood or Jesus Christ or Batman, turn back the earth, save the blonde from King Kong, and leave only a silver bullet behind.

"Control of behavior through the ideological production of unfulfillable desire," Ann called that, but knowing it didn't make any difference. Ten minutes talking to Edward, and I'd be flushed and trembling, have to go outside and lie down on the grass. I heard rumors about him, that he was unpredictable, praised you one year and attacked you the next, and that he had affairs with students — news which, far from putting me off, tortured me with envy and hope.

But in his presence I could only chatter, or fall mute as a rock, and I assumed that he was laughing at me. Once I saw him at a play and confessed my devotion to Shakespeare, a trifle fulsomely. He looked down at me from a great height.

"The boy had talent," he said, and walked away.

◆◇◆

One day he called me at home and asked me out to lunch. We sat upstairs at Larry Blake's, in a private corner, drinking white wine. When we finished our club sandwiches, he gazed into my eyes. Suddenly he reached across the table, holding out his hand.

I stared at it in amazement, and my heart went flat. His palm was soft and damp, and little drops of sweat shone on his forehead. His eyes seemed depthless and intent, like a lizard's. Numbly I took his hand, and he squeezed it, mouth opening in a wordless grimace.

"Meet me tomorrow afternoon?" he murmured

as we were walking back, crossing a crowded street. I stared at him mutely, and he gave a decisive nod. "That's the next thing."

I reasoned with myself. I'd wanted this man for years. Even if, for some reason, that were no longer true, I still admired him more than anyone I knew, and here was my chance to know him as few people did. Of course, he probably realized how I'd been mooning over him, and what would happen if I backed out now?

Meanly, crassly, I thought about my dissertation. My heart shrivelled to a pebble. It was too late to change directors — I'd prepared myself in Edward's special field. I'd made the acquaintance of a pile of books and learned to sound like I was intimate with lots of others. I'd endured twelve graduate seminars, a whole summer of round-the-clock Greek, years of humiliation at the hands of supercilious native speakers of German and French, as well as fourteen hours of doctoral exams, all of which qualified me for exactly nothing if I never wrote my dissertation. Surely I was only having an attack of nerves.

"All right," I said.

Strolling back between rows of monkey trees on Sproul Plaza, he kept a decorous distance away. Fumbling for the key to his office, his fingers shook, and his eyes were wet. He glanced up and down the hallway to make sure no one was watching, and locked the door behind us. He loomed over me. Bending down, holding his lips stiff, he pressed them into mine, as if trying to achieve a good weld.

The next day we met in a room he had rented on the Northside, asking me to bring sheets. Without touching me he stripped off his clothes and hung them over a chair. My previous lovers had all worn boxer shorts or nothing under their jeans, but he had on white fitted briefs of the same flimsy jersey as his v-neck undershirt, and the way they stretched across his lean shanks was the least erotic sight I had ever seen.

This is E. W. Hooper getting into bed with you, I reminded myself. I tried to remember any one of those thousand steamy dreams. He turned out to be a good lover, in waking life, narrow of range (certain acts "never happen in our house," he said) but very enthusiastic. Afterwards we lay in bed for hours, talking and laughing in a way I had never imagined. He told amusing stories about his colleagues, his children, his wife. His wife had started ignoring him, he said, when the children were born, and had perfected it in recent years. He had been faithful to her for two decades, but lately he had not been once or twice. He seemed to listen raptly to everything I said. We made love again and talked under the covers until he had to go home.

I didn't expect to hear from him for at least a week, but that night he called me three times, once when his wife took out the garbage and twice after she fell asleep.

"I love you," he whispered, with amazed intensity. "I can't live without you. When can I see you again?"

We met again the next day, and the day after that, and a year later we were still meeting every afternoon, making love more than once and talking for hours. I stopped working on my dissertation — it didn't matter, I was getting my philosophy in bed. The campus went on strike, and Edward started meeting his classes in the evenings, at his house. When it was time to meet me at our room, he'd tell his wife he was going to the office, and never have to cross the picket lines.

I was certainly in love with him by that time, if I hadn't been before, and between us there was something that passed for a life. He called me every few hours around the clock and wrote me hundreds of tiny pencilled notes. I'd find them tucked like cookie-fortunes into my birth-control pills ("The error is not to fall, but to fall from no height"), at random dates on my pocket calendar ("10 p.m. Edward loves Laura. 10:10 p.m. Edward still loves Laura"). He wrote so small he could put a disquisition on a cigarette (about the shortness of life, its burning, its light) or a Tampax wrapper (about the shortness of life, its secrecy, its loss). The Sayings of Hoo Pa, I called such remarks. When he had to leave town, he sent me a Burma Shave series of telegrams: (1) "I can live without jazz." (2) "I can live without roast beef." (3) "But I cannot live without you." (4) "(Plutarch weeps!)"

I assumed he wanted to leave his wife, and that it would happen whether I wanted it or not. I made my way to our room past shattered storefront windows and lines of police in riot shields, crowds screaming in the background when they dropped tear gas. I did not watch the news, because I didn't want to know about children's skin burned off by napalm, ministers shot in motel parking lots. As far as I could tell, the world was coming to an end. Why should Edward's marriage be any exception?

He never said as much, but I saw signs that he wanted to be with me all the time. Our room was in an old stucco house, covered with bougainvillea, gnarled vines that grew right over the windows, making them into leafy rooms for birds. Lying in bed we could watch whole cycles of pigeon love inside. They'd eye each other and crane their necks, until one suddenly hopped the other and madly humped. Seconds later, they'd leap apart and sit stunned. They built their nests directly onto the windowsill and sat on the eggs for weeks, but we never saw any fledglings hatched. One day we'd look out, and the eggs would be gone. The nests were always too flimsy, and the eggs fell out.

"Pathetic fallacy," I reminded him, but he gazed at me with tragic eyes.

❖❖❖

As we moved into our second year, it occurred to me that he was not actually planning to leave his wife.

"That's right," he said when I mentioned it. He could never do that to her — after all, he'd promised he'd always be there. They had friends in common, children, a life. He'd have to give up everything, in particular his wife, whom he did, by the way, love. In fact, he was only managing the guilt so long as she didn't know, and if she ever found out, it would have to end.

Everything felt a little different after that. Leaving our room, I started to wonder who had heard us, and how much they knew. I envied people on the street. I got to be a little too interested in Edward's wife. I made him talk about her, more than he liked. I tried to realize what it meant, that he'd been sleeping next to her all my life.

One day I followed her. I was on my way to meet him when I saw her, taking pictures in Sproul Plaza, and I kept him waiting for an hour while I watched. She was small and quick and self-absorbed, in khaki pants and a leather jacket, blond hair in a ponytail. She searched the crowd as she rewound, spotted her next target, put the camera to her face, rewound. She never asked permission, but once I saw her flash a strong grin at something someone said. The loudspeaker was booming, and the crowd took up a chant — "Death to the killers," or something like that. She never noticed me behind her, even when I followed closely. I stared at the back of her neck. He knows that skin, I thought. He knows the smell of that hair.

When I got the infection, I knew it had the makings of an ultimatum. I made my first trip to Dr. Burke, and Edward and I took the pills. I was glad when we seemed to be cured — no use forcing any issues, I assured myself. But then it came back. Secretly I hoped that Dr. Burke would find a way, that we could take some other pill and go on as we were. Even so, the day before I went to see her again, I played my cards: I mentioned to Edward that he might have to choose. If he couldn't arrange to give his wife the pills, we might be forced to part. Unless of course he was planning to stop making love to his wife.

"Oh." His face flushed, then drained to gray. His eyes got wet. "You seem awfully eager for this to be over. Why don't you at least wait to talk to the doctor?"

•◆•◆•◆•

I stepped out of the student health center, clutching my new vial of pills. The day was warm, breezy and blue, the kind that would mean spring in Cambridge but any time at all in Berkeley, where the camellias bloom in January and crocuses come up three times a year, exhausted and confused.

Leaving campus, I avoided Sproul Plaza. It was close to noon, and soon students would be offering themselves by hecatombs to the police. Faintly on the breeze came the shouting of a lone voice. I could still hear it as I reached my street, the boom of language, though not what it meant.

The house I lived in was a peeling Victorian, with weathered gingerbread and five kinds of fruit trees in the yard, including a guava, a date palm and one my housemates insisted was a banana. Lately they had decided to secede from the union. They answered the phone "Banana Republic," and Ann had made a flag, with a pig rampant, "*Don't Tread On Me*" embroidered across the bottom — limply it hung from the front porch. As a step toward economic independence, Buzzy and Pete were hoeing up the yard to plant a garden. Weeks after the start of excavation, there was still no sign of horticulture, but the churned dirt gave off a cool scent of root rot in the noonday air.

I opened the mailbox by the gate from habit, not because I expected anything to be in there. My housemates watched our borders and the mailman's every move, and if anyone put anything in the box, they ran a bomb check on it in the first few minutes.

This time, however, they'd missed something: a Philosophy Department envelope, fat with pages, my name pencilled on the front. He must have delivered it by hand, before the house was up. I tore it open, read the first line ("How eager you are to put an end to this!") and took it up to the sagging front porch.

I sat on the top step and unfolded it. The writing was nothing like his usual precise print — it was jaggedly scrawled, in ballpoint pen, the tip dug hard into three sheets of unlined paper, slanting off the page and slashed with exclamation marks. I skimmed it quickly, trying not to take it in, just to locate the major landmines and antipersonnel devices. I had "dismissed him," he said, "with casual savagery." I was "shallow," "selfish," my "emotions stalled at age thirteen." I only wanted a man until he loved me, and then as far as I was concerned "he can just drop dead!!" He wondered "where it would end," since I had done it to "so many others," including "two husbands" and "countless lovers."

I read it again, carefully. Two husbands, countless lovers. I was twenty-five years old, and he'd known me since I was twenty-one. When did he think I'd ravished all those other men?

"We will probably meet in the future," the letter went on. "But do not expect me to be able to speak to you. I promise not to try to reach you, and I expect you to do the same for me. I know you think you can shrug me off and I'll still be there, but I'm only a slow learner. Even the detached leg of a cockroach can be taught to pull itself out of sugar water, when you shock it enough times in that solution."

❖❖❖

My housemates were in the living room. Pete was holding the baby, walking her around the room, and Buzzy was watching him, while Ann knelt on the rug, throwing the I Ching. Their faces were fresh and pink, since they had lately risen from various beds — two of them, if not all three, from Ann's.

"Wooo-eeeeee," Pete sang. He lifted the baby up and bent her over backwards, one hand under her head, until her wisp of hair nearly brushed the rug. "Weeeeee-oooooo."

"Easy, man," Buzzy said.

Buzzy was just back from Vietnam and learning to play the sitar. Pete was 4F, because of surfer's knots on his feet, and studying to be a mailman. They lived by barter and yard fruit, as did Ann — Buzzy's pension paid the rent, and Ann's ADC usually went to the Black Panthers. By now they should be girding themselves in boots and leather jackets and Che Guevara berets, strapping on the baby and heading down to Sproul. But Pete was barefooted in jeans, and Buzzy sat on a barstool, smoking, wearing nothing but yoga pants and a woven leather thong around one wrist. Ann looked like something by Botticelli: her yellow hair was rayed out in a WASP natural, and she had wrapped herself in an apricot Indian bedspread, like a sarong, plumping up her already quite full breasts. I'd known her since we went to mass in pillbox hats and white gloves, mortified at the thought that our knees might be showing under our skirts. I wore the occasional miniskirt now and no longer owned a bra, but Ann had gone way beyond most of us on the question of breasts. She displayed hers like a national treasure, and nursed on the front porch.

"Examine the living words and not the dead ones," she said, bending over the white translucent stones.

"Hey-ey-ey," Buzzy called, apparently to me, but without taking his eyes off Pete.

"Woooo-eeeeee," Pete sang, tipping the baby over again. The baby laughed, her face half grin, a click of hysterical mirth in her throat.

"Hey, easy, man," Buzzy said.

Buzzy and Pete were both devoted to childcare. When Simone de Beauvoir cried at night, Buzzy or Pete would get up and go to Ann's room to help. Sometimes the other would already be there, or they would both show up at once, and then there would be long discussions, lights left burning half the night. Sometimes I caught sight of the three of them, asleep in starlike configurations, fully clothed, on various beds.

Once when Buzzy and Ann retired upstairs to bed, Pete went out into the garden and worked for hours in the dark, to give them space. "*Space,*" he said, when I went out to talk to him, and hacked into the ground with a hoe. "*Space* is the whole problem of Western civilization. *Space* is something we make into prisons, instead of room to grow."

"We're trying to do away with the yang side of love," Ann once said. "But it keeps creeping back in." Sometimes she gave soothing talks on the beauty of not owning anyone or anything. She didn't own Simone de Beauvoir, and if her daughter wanted to call herself Marilyn Monroe when she grew up, that would be all right. "Names, walls, property, laws — nothing but obstructions to the flow." She'd be happy to call the rest of us anything we liked.

"Laura's home early," Buzzy said. He made a fist around the cigarette, tapped his knuckles on the ashtray. "Maybe she's decided to join us. Maybe she's decided that today's the day."

"Tranquillity," Ann said, beaming, as she lifted her head from the stones. "Gentleness of spirit. Nothing hard or frictional today."

Buzzy nodded at me. "Good day to trip."

"Hey, hey, Laura's home, is she going to trip?" Pete sang, swinging the baby over again.

"Hey, Pete," Buzzy called. "You know, that wee child just ate herself a fair amount, not long ago."

Pete crooned, kissing her head. "And did she just eat her tiny lunch? Is that a fact? Is that what the tiny person just did? Then we'll have to be careful, won't we? Yes indeedy do." He held her head up near his own and danced her around the room.

I had the smallest room in the house, just off the kitchen, but it had the advantage of being close enough to the phone that the cord would reach inside.

I smoked two cigarettes fast, to get up a head of nicotine nerve. Fingers vibrating, I dialed Edward's house. I had never talked to his wife, never even heard her voice. What was I going to say if she picked it up?

"Hello," he said slowly, ironically, mocking the whole idea. His voice was large and wide, broad and deep. Behind him I heard the thunk of a refrigerator door.

"It's me. I've only been married once. I can count my lovers."

"Yes, well, my office hours are Tuesday and Thursday, two to four. If you'll stop by then —"

"Okay, maybe I haven't been a model mistress, maybe I haven't said I'll do this forever, but if we're going to talk about the domestic virtues —"

"Yes, well, if you'll just put the paper in my box — do you know where that is? Moses Hall —"

"As for love, you've got to admit I've done a decent imitation of it for a year or two, and it seems to me the burden of proof —"

". . . second floor — the department office. That's right. You're welcome." He hung up.

My housemates had moved out onto the back lawn, and I didn't have to lie about where I was going. My feet were already aching from the morning's walk, but I took off as fast as possible toward the Northside. Surely he would go to our room now — I wasn't going to consider the other possibilities. He would be on his way to our room now.

A chopper was ack-acking up near Sproul, and waves of screams blew past when the wind was right. I cut across the west end of the campus. The Northside was an uphill climb, and to get to our room I had to march up a block like a wall, on Arch.

I paused often to breathe and sat down twice. To compose myself, I smoked three cigarettes. I watched for him on the street. He would be riding his son's motorcycle — he felt invisible on the bike, because no one would expect him to ride one. He always wore a helmet with a tinted visor and left it on until he was safe inside.

The bike was not parked in its usual place, down the block, or anywhere near the old stucco house. Ducking under the bougainvillea, I went around to the back and started to climb the plain pine stairs.

The door of our room was open. Out of it came a stench of disinfectant, the clank of a mop against pail. The mattress was bare, a woman's broad back bent over beyond it in a pink-flowered shift. On the top step, in a brown paper bag, were our sheets and towels.

❖❖❖

The afternoon light slanted down, hot and bright. Red hibiscus and pink camellias ruffled in the wind, and in the distance the blue bay sparkled. From the height of the hill on Arch, I could see smoke drifting toward the hills, from campus. Gunshots popped, and three helicopters tipped and darted, hacking. Sirens echoed off the hills.

Going down the hill, my heels threw me forward, crushing my toes — I reached down, snatched them off and chucked them into the street. Standing hot and dirty on the sidewalk, I tried to light my last cigarette — it broke in half. I ripped the package open and threw it as hard as I could. Catching the wind, it blew back, landed at my feet.

I limped out into the street to pick up my shoes. They had landed by an ambulance parked with its back end gaping.

The doors of the nearest apartment house flew open and two men rushed out, carrying a stretcher, a girl strapped down on it, lolling unconscious in a flimsy robe, legs open. All down the insides of her legs was blood, half sponged off, half dried, red on beige like damasked flowers. She rolled side to side as they lifted the stretcher and shoved it inside. Slam, slam, went the doors. The ambulance sped off.

Sometime later, I made my way home. Gritty smoke was drifting over our house as I limped up the walk. Ann and the others were out on the unchurned portion of the back lawn. They'd lashed the baby's basket in a tree and strung up madras bedspreads to make a tent, inside which all three reclined. Buzzy embraced his wine-dark sitar, while Ann and Pete lay against large pillows, her head on his chest, his bare feet out in the late sun.

Ann stood up and came out to meet me. She put her arms around me, smelling of patchouli and baby powder. "Your aura is in tatters. Come into the tent. Don't worry. We have what you need. We'll take care of you now."

I lay back against the pillows, and Ann rubbed baby oil into my feet. She started to knead them.

"The map of the sole is the map of the soul. Come out, come out, spirit that binds Laura's feet."

Pete brought me a glass of cranberry juice, brilliant red in the sun. "Eat me, drink me," he said, holding out his palm.

Ann worked my feet like clay. "Don't think about it. Your mind is free — just let it go."

I looked at it. It was a pink flake, tiny and translucent — it didn't look as if it could do much harm. I put it in my mouth.

"Good," Ann said, smiling into my eyes. She massaged my ankles. "Now, just let go. You're in the hands of the universe now."

For a long time, nothing in particular happened. The sides of the tent sighed in the breeze, like Valentino's in *The Sheik*. Smoke shredded across the sky and blew away. Buzzy thumped and plucked his overgrown guitar. It was crowded in the tent, all four of us cramped together like children under a table. After a while, Ann stopped massaging my feet.

"Well, thanks," I said, sitting up. "I think I'll go inside now. I guess I'm not very susceptible."

"Oh no!" they cried, laughing, pulling me back down. "Stay here, don't go anywhere right now."

The space in the tent got even smaller. My visual field now appeared to be a movie screen, with black around the edges. It was the screen that was getting smaller — I was moving back from it, into black space. Everything I could see was shrinking with distance, becoming tiny, including my arms and legs. They were so far off now, in a moment they would detach. Frantically I waved them, to make them more visible. I could just make out the tiny quivering motion.

"Blast off," a gnat's voice said, miles away.

❖◆❖

A nun in khaki consulted her clipboard and made an impatient gesture. I was only making trouble — I had agreed to die, it had been my choice. The warp and woof of the universe had shifted, reorganizing matter and life. What was left was an infinite grid. If I felt I couldn't breathe, it was because I had no lungs.

Neither did anyone else. The grass, the trees, the people were gone, because of what I did. Voices sang the *Kyrie eleison* of the Mozart *Requiem,* over and over, with malicious intent.

I opened my eyes in a place without seasons or depth. Bodies sprawled on the grass, continuous with the web of everything. They lay at odd angles, washed in monotonous gold light.

I tried to sit up but could not. I tried and tried. I felt them come to life: cells of muscle, one by one. Cells of bone. Cells of fascia, nerve and blood. They put my feet on the ground.

"Don't try to walk," the voices sang, sweetly, a choral round. "Don't try, don't try, don't try to do that again. Never again, never again, you'll never do that again."

I got one foot off the ground and balanced on the other. I swung the lifted leg out, wavered, gripped the muscles in my planted leg and did not fall. Lowering my toes, I shifted my weight, experimentally, ounce by ounce. I balanced again.

I could see the kitchen stoop. Beside it crouched a camellia bush, black-green armored leaves becoming spears, becoming hands. I did not look. I swung the other leg out, into air.

I was beside the bush. I lifted one bare foot, feeling for the stair. Suddenly Ann was there above me, grinning and smirking.

"Out of my way, assassin," I said. "I'm not going to die."

She stood back and let me by.

❖·❖·❖

I organized a pot of coffee and drank it all. I stood in a long cold shower, then a hot one, then more cold. I put on clean clothes.

Something was wrong with the shape of my room, one corner of the ceiling punched in toward the middle instead of out into space, but I ignored that. I sat at my desk, holding the phone on my lap. Everything had to be put back exactly the way it was before. I stared down at a book. I was alert in a way that I had never been, but I could not read a line.

Long after dark, I heard the others come inside. The music throbbed. They knocked on my door from time to time, but I did not answer, and the door was locked. After a while, the music stopped. I heard them go upstairs.

The vial of pills was on my desk — eight at bedtime, it said. It was bedtime now, though I didn't think I'd ever sleep again. I wasn't going to take them. He was going to call, and we would take them together. What he'd done today was the panic that precedes the break. I held on to the phone.

Something rustled in the bushes, outside my window, too loud and deliberate to be a raccoon. I flicked off the light and sat in the dark, my heart thudding hard.

A shadow fell on the curtain — a head, big as a minotaur's. A huge fist rose and knocked on the window. A deep voice whispered, "Laura."

I ran to the back door and stood on the stoop. Rustling toward me through the bushes, he looked very tall in his round white helmet. I couldn't see his face.

I held out my arms. "It's not too late." I had the pills in my hand.

"Wait," he whispered, and gripped my arm.

He pulled me along, toward the street. My feet were bare, but he held me up, and I scarcely felt the cold cement. The night was clear, silver light and black shadows. Streetlight shone on palm fronds and garbage-can lids. It was quiet, except for a dog's bark, silly with distance.

The motorcycle stood at the curb. He stopped beside it and took off his helmet. Streetlight shone in his eyes. Taking hold of his head, I kissed him gently, the way I'd taught him. He unzipped his jacket, fingers trembling slightly.

"Ella's been watching me all day, I don't know why," he whispered. "By the time you called I'd already said I was staying home, and I couldn't think of a reason to get away. Finally I just went out the window. I have to get back, before she finds out."

He took a flat paper bag out of his jacket and handed it to me.

"I wonder if you'd mind keeping these for me. I don't know why I didn't think of it sooner. When I was young, no man ever went anywhere without one of these in his wallet. But you've probably never even seen one."

He was right about one thing: I'd never seen one before. I opened the bag. Inside were blue cellophane strips of detachable squares. In each square something coiled, something pale and tender and gleaming, like a fetal salamander. They were waiting to hatch, when the time was right, each one exactly the same as the last: a temporary compromise with blight, like every day of the rest of my life.

ASSUMED
IDENTITY

❖❖❖

IT HAPPENED ALMOST every time he fell asleep: another dream of tragic fucking. Sometimes it was Laura, which made a certain sense. But it could be anyone: colleagues, graduate students, even once in a while his wife. This time it was a neighbor he'd never found attractive. (He reviewed the scenes, glad they hadn't actually happened.) It was ridiculous the way he cared, no matter who she was. There they'd be, moaning and writhing, on a beach or a hillside. Then suddenly she'd be gone, and he'd be desperate to find her.

He sat up and ran his hands over his head — he'd slept in his clothes again, on the sweaty leather couch in his study. He washed his face with cold water, avoiding the sight in the mirror — he knew what he'd see. He would have faded another shade: not only his hair but his eyebrows, his skin, even his lips, bleaching like an overexposed photograph. He was fifty, and fading fast. There would be no need for cancer, or coma, parts of himself cut out or twisted into knots and bursting open. In a year or two, he would simply be invisible.

When the doorbell rang, he listened to the house but heard no footsteps. It was noon by now, and Ella would be down on campus, stalking hippies and National Guardsmen with her camera. He took his time drying his face — he wasn't expecting anyone. The bell rang once more before he hung up the towel.

The young man whirled awkwardly when Edward opened the door — he had been leaning back, examining the house, in khaki pants, a green polo shirt and aviator sunglasses, a clipboard under his arm. Recovering his balance, he examined Edward, from his unshaven cheeks to the wornout loafers on his feet.

"Professor Hooper?" In the man's quick clipped drawl, this came out "Prafessah Hoopah?" Flipping open his wallet with one hand, he held it out. "Andrew Hodges, sir, FBI. I wonder if I could trouble you with a few questions."

Edward held his palm out like a traffic signal. "This way," he said and closed the door behind him.

When Hodges didn't move, he walked ahead of him, up the front walk to the driveway, and climbed to the street. He didn't know why, exactly, but he didn't want to talk to this man in his house. "Why didn't you call my office?"

Hodges caught up with him, dropping his voice conspiratorily. "I could have done that, Professor. And I will next time, if you prefer. I understand how you might feel a little . . . I just thought you might be home, with the campus on strike the way it is, and all."

Edward turned and strode uphill, away from the house of the neighbor he'd dreamed about. The street was high on the Berkeley ridge, with a view out over the bay, all the way to San Francisco and the Golden Gate. Today the sun was bright and hot, but the view was lightly veiled in white haze. It was September, the end of the long dry season, and a smell of singe hung in the air, from forests burning in the Sierra.

He set a pace he thought might be a little stiff for Hodges, who was not tall. He looked at the view over Hodges' head. "Classes haven't started yet."

Hodges was keeping up, striding manfully along. "Oh, so you will be meeting your classes? Even with the strike and all?"

"Is *that* what this is about?"

"No, sir. Not actually. I just wondered if we were right in assuming you might be home."

Edward wished he'd brought his pipe — when he wanted to avoid answering, he could do so pointedly, scraping it out, examining it, blowing into it. He'd been trying to smoke it less, on doctor's advice, and he missed it badly. He sank his hands in his pockets and picked up the pace.

Hodges caught up to him, panting slightly. "Well. What it *is* about, actually — it's about your son, Heinrich. We're trying to locate him. We thought you might be able to help us."

Hank was their third, named for Ella's father, and no one had ever called him Heinrich. Edward looked down at the little man. He was an anemic blond, skinny and pale and ratlike. He had red pitted scars on his cheeks, like gravel in cement.

"What did you do, look at his birth certificate?"

Hodges tried to consult his clipboard, but Edward did not slow down. "Yes, sir. I believe it was — was it Cambridge, Massachusetts, December 1948? Mother a German alien."

Edward resisted the urge to tell the man to go to hell. Thirty years before, during the war, the FBI had investigated Ella, on suspicion of being German. "Alien's a bit strong, don't you think? Why don't you say refugee?"

Hodges' voice was patient. "It's just a legal term, sir — because she wasn't a citizen. Still isn't, I believe. Now, as far as Heinrich is concerned, it would be a help to us if you could tell us when was the last time you saw him, and where he lived then."

Edward kept his eyes focussed ahead. "What do you want with my son?"

"Well, sir, I'm afraid I'd rather not say. It's nothing to worry about. Not yet, anyway."

He tried to stop, but Edward kept walking. "I'll be the judge of that."

Hodges caught up. "Well, sir, I was hoping to keep this from you. I didn't want to worry you unnecessarily. But the fact is, what we want to talk to him about — what it has to do with — is that shooting at the courthouse, over in Marin, last May."

Edward stopped. "You think he was mixed up in the Angela Davis case?"

Hodges gave him a knowing smile. "That's what the papers call it, but that's not what we call it. And it's not that we think Heinrich was involved with it, necessarily. However —" He flipped up the papers on his board, slid out an 8 × 10 black and white. "This is your son, isn't it?"

It was a good picture of Hank, the way he'd looked the last few years: hair down to his waist, unwashed, a calm and earnest expression. He was looking straight at the camera, through a screen, with Ella's large pale eyes. The room was bare, a man in uniform against one wall. On the near side of the screen was a black man, his back turned, hunched over, his head near Hank's.

Hodges leaned in close to point, smelling of Brylcreem and aftershave. "That's San Quentin, last year. This gentleman here — he's the one that held the rifle while it was taped to the judge's neck." He put two fingers on the photograph, waiting politely until Edward let it go. He slid it back into the envelope. "We don't know what your son was doing there. We just want to ask him a few questions, before he leaves the country."

Edward's breath caught. "What do you mean, leaves the country?"

Hodges watched him carefully. "You really didn't know about that, did you. That surprises me. Well, yes. It seems he's planning to take a little trip. To Cuba. Some of his friends went over there last year, and now they've arranged it for him, to help him out of this tight spot he's in. Venceremos Brigade, they call themselves. They like to go over and pick the sugar cane, and sing 'We Shall Overcome' . . ."

◆◇◆◇◆

The only number he had for Hank was written in the back of the book he was carrying the last time Edward saw him. Hank had made him promise not to write it in the family phone book or even tell Ella that he had it. It was not where he lived but rather someone who could give him a message, in an emergency. Edward had written it down, assuming that Hank was simply in a mobile phase, unemployed and sleeping on friends' couches, hiding out from one of his many girls.

He went to his study and pulled it down — it was in Michael Polanyi, *Personal Knowledge*. He started to dial. Abruptly he stopped and pushed the button down. It might be bugged. "Baaaaaaaaaaaaaaaa," said the phone, not at all a neutral sound. He put the receiver down.

With one of the other children, he would have assumed the FBI was wrong, but with Hank it was not so easy — Hank had never conformed to his parents' expectations. When he was born, Edward was writing his dissertation, the older boys were trying to put out each other's eyes, and a high wind was blowing through Ella, over one failure or another of his own. Hank helped out by crying around the clock, pausing only when pushed in the stroller. Edward had to walk him all over town, with a book propped open on the hood of the buggy, and as soon as he stopped walking, Hank would wail again.

The others grew fast into big hardy kids who played rough and dropped to sleep like buckets down a well, but Hank stayed delicate as a frog, with an intense stare. At night he climbed out of his crib and wandered the house, and he wore diapers until the age of four. He seemed to have too much imagination: he believed the mailman was going to steal him and send him on a spaceship to San Jose, and that if he fell asleep, he might wake up in the morning as a mouse. Nothing could reassure him: he did not believe what he was told. Long after he was clear on anatomy, he drew pictures of girls with penises under their dresses, and referred to certain males as "she."

"Some grandfathers are girls," he explained, in spite of his brothers' glee.

He did not approve of kindergarten, or first grade, or second — left at school, he would simply walk away. Finally they sent him to a private tutor, who discovered that he did approve of languages. While his brothers played softball, basketball, soccer, Hank learned German, French, and Latin. He affected a grave adult manner and made up multilingual puns, delivered without a trace of humor. While his brothers perfected their cannonballs and blasted AM rock, he listened to Mozart and Charlie Parker, and learned to play the saxophone. He demanded a tuxedo at the age of ten and stole Edward's ties to wear to junior high. He cut most of high school and spent his days in the university library, reading Freud, Marx and Sartre in the original.

"Have you seen Marx on that?" he would delicately ask Edward. "You might not have — it's in a rather obscure manuscript."

He won a scholarship to Berkeley in an essay

contest, writing a Marxist critique of the Rat Man case, but he had to take the high-school-equivalency test to get in, and he flunked it twice, since he had never learned to add, subtract, or divide.

When the boys reached a certain age, Edward and Ella tried to treat them as adults, declining to interfere in their sexual lives, and Hank took on that policy as a challenge. One evening when he was seventeen he brought home a black woman who must have been five years older than he was and a foot taller. She shook Edward's hand and looked him coolly in the eye. Her hair was all in cornrows, and she was wearing combat fatigues.

"Mom, Dad," Hank said. "It's time you met my comrade, Anasi."

Very nice to meet you, Edward and Ella said, and watched them go upstairs. Hank's bed was over the kitchen table, and for the next two hours the ceiling rocked, the house filled with Hank's happy yelps. When they finally came down, he made Anasi sit at the table while he padded around in his bare feet, glowing and joking as he fixed them both a snack. Catching sight of his mother's ashen face, he placed an arm gently around her shoulders.

"It's difficult, isn't it? Knowing that someone is having so much fun, somewhere in the house. It used to drive me crazy when I was a kid, listening to you and Dad."

He moved out shortly after that, and he hadn't been home since. Sometimes Edward saw him on campus, picketing Sproul Hall or passing out leaflets under Sather Gate. He'd grin when he saw Edward and give the victory sign. "*Viva la revolución!*" he might call, with a look that implied this was a wonderful joke between them.

Sometimes he'd stroll into his father's office and lecture him in a quiet voice. He had a plainer style these days, since he'd dropped out of school and joined the People's Labor Party. He never used foreign words or allusions to difficult texts, and he always wore the same beat-up jean jacket.

"Ethics are capitalist and reactionary," he said once, holding up Edward's second book. "History and becoming are revolutionary. Look, I know what you think. You think that every attempt to make things better ends in Stalin, and how many millions dead? So you don't commit yourself. You stand back and watch, as if it were possible to *do nothing*. Or maybe you think you've already tried, and failed, and that failure clears responsibility, the way bankruptcy clears debt. Only stop to consider: what if you haven't actually failed?"

The last time he'd seen Hank was at a bar in Oakland called The Pigeon, where Hank had asked him to come. The place was full of people, all of them black, laughing and eating big plates of food.

When Hank came in, it was not through the front door but from the kitchen or somewhere else in back. He looked thinner than Edward remembered, his hair in a flat braid down his back. Sitting across from him in the booth, the gold light from the bar reached no lower than his black beret, but his eyes shone dimly in the shadow as he studied his father. He didn't want to talk about himself, he said. He didn't want to criticize. He was only puzzled.

"I just want to ask you one more time. Okay, so you're a bourgeois individualist — so are all the rest of us. But you and I both know you've never been happy with things as they are. You keep up the bourgeois appearances, but you escape through loopholes. And I've always assumed that wasn't as far as you'd be willing to go. After all, it's just a solution for yourself, it doesn't do a thing for anyone else. When it came down to it, I thought, you'd be on our side." He smacked the table with his palm. "Was I so wrong?"

◆◆◆

Edward did not feel obliged to explain himself to Hank. He might be on Hank's side in many ways, and even on the PLP's in one or two. But he didn't want Hank to overestimate the real-world effect of what he was trying to do.

"On your side in what?" was all he'd said, and he hoped the message had gotten through.

He went upstairs to Hank's old room, which had a view of the street, and looked out the window. A hundred yards down on the other side was a plain American car, institutional green. Inside sat two heavy men in brown suits and flattop haircuts, looking so much like FBI, they probably weren't. Stoically they watched him as he regarded them.

He'd better take the motorcycle — a person could be almost invisible on a bike. He'd promised to keep it running while David was gone — David was his second son, now in Vietnam. The first year, he'd ridden it every afternoon, disguised in David's black leather jacket and space-explorer helmet, to get to the room where he met Laura. Since that time, he'd hardly touched the bike at all.

After a short search, he found the helmet and jacket. The leather jacket had an unpleasantly fatty feel, like raw bacon — he put it on, but tried not to breathe it in. He got the bike out of the garage. To get to the street he had to pass the green car, but he put on the helmet and ran hard, hoping they wouldn't know who he was. He didn't stop until he was out of sight around the bend.

The start always gave him trouble — the smooth soles of his shoes kept sliding off. David wore black leather boots with heels for this procedure, but nothing could induce Edward to take the outfit that far. Over and over he reared up and threw himself down on the starter. Finally the engine fired, destroying birdsong and concentration for blocks around.

It was a big bike, heavy as a boulder, and he tried to humor it. Avoiding his own block, he threaded slowly through the streets downhill, remembering how to lean into the curves, how soon to brake. As he dropped toward campus, Virginia Street rose up to meet him. Here was where he used to turn, uphill, to the room where he met Laura. He'd heel the bike far over and glide around the turn, smooth as a hull in water, then speed up just enough to rise one block and float to a stop under a mimosa. He kept his eyes front, driving past the corner.

The black leather jacket was hot, and at the next stop sign he took it off, squeezed it down as far as it would go and snapped it under the clip on the back of the bike. He would look more like himself in his button-down shirt, but it hardly mattered — no one was following him. He found a phone booth and dialed the number he had for his son.

"We don't know anyone named Hank or Heinrich or anything Hooper," a woman said on the other end. "I told you that already."

"I haven't talked to you before. This really is his father."

"Mother-fucking pig," she said and hung up the phone.

He drove around the campus to the Southside. In the student neighborhood near Telegraph, he found the last house Hank had lived in — it was a commune then, and some of the same people might be around. He didn't think he was being followed, but just to be sure he circled the block, pulled into the driveway of the house behind it, and cut through their backyard. He swung his leg over a low fence buried in honeysuckle that divided the yards. Hank's old house was brown-shingled, three stories high, wisteria vines clutching its sides. The windows were open, no screens, torn yellow shades luffing in the breeze.

He knocked on the unpainted back door. Upstairs, someone took three steps near a window and stopped. He could make out only the corner of a bureau in the dark beyond the shade. Whoever was up there did not answer when he knocked again.

He rode back toward campus. He knew Hank wouldn't be there, but he didn't know where else to look. Hank was trying now to organize the workers' revolution, compared to which, he said, the student protests would seem a tantrum. He spent his time in Salinas, Delano, Fruitvale, and a lot of other towns where Edward had never been.

He parked the bike and walked up Telegraph,

carrying the helmet. Squatters lined the sidewalk, bare feet black, under storefront windows boarded with plywood. On one corner a young man shouted that the earth, the earth, how could anyone think they owned it? A young girl asked Edward for money, and two youths tried to sell him belts. A thin man touched his arm and silently handed him a leaflet. Inside, it listed all the women who had wronged him, starting with his mother, who had given him synthetic formula, and ending with the name of a girl who had aborted his child in Mexico.

Cars trolled by, windshields flashing in the sun. At the next corner the light changed against him, and he had to wait at the curb. Into his line of sight slid the roof of a green car. The men in brown suits turned their heads in unison to gaze at him, eyes drifting down to the motorcycle helmet cradled against his side.

"You want this?" he said and shoved the helmet at the next kid asking for money.

It was a quiet day on campus, no microphone in Sproul. He loitered along, searching faces. The sun was bright and high, glancing off fliers, hand-lettered posters, suntanned skin. At the end of the row of tables, under the green bronze arch of Sather Gate, a tall black woman in a jean jacket and black beret handed him a leaflet. *"Position of the Worker-Student Coalition on the Bombing of Cambodia,"* it read.

"Anasi?" he said, holding the folded sheet.

She went on passing out leaflets. Her hair was now in tiny intricate braids, looping around her head.

"Remember me? Edward Hooper. You came to my house one time."

She smiled slowly, without looking at him. "I remember your house. I remember the whole street. One fortress after another, each one with a man and a woman locked up inside. Two by two, like Noah's Ark."

"That's the place. Listen Can you tell Hank to call me?"

Abruptly she turned and walked away, so fast she was nearly to Telegraph before he caught her. He grabbed her arm. "Does that mean you will? Look, I just need to talk to him."

She shook off his hand. "I never heard of him, or you." She crossed to Telegraph and was gone.

❖❖❖

He held down the throttle, pressed his face into the wind, let it blow back his eyelids. The lip of his drive was blind. You couldn't see if anything was parked in it, and usually he paused at the top to look, but this time he didn't even slow down. He roared over the top, dropped off the edge and plummeted to the garage.

Hodges was on the deck, back turned, examining

the view. "Goddamnit," Edward said, and got off the bike.

At the top of the steps, he stopped. The man on the deck was young and blond, but even from the back he was better-looking than Hodges, healthier, with smooth skin. The hair was lighter, almost white, and cut so close the scalp showed pink. The khaki pants were right, but the polo shirt was navy blue. The young man turned, mirrored sunglasses where his eyes should be, and stood without moving, giving nothing away by gesture. Edward was almost touching him before he knew for certain that it was Hank.

"Jesus Christ." He gripped Hank's arm, wanting to throw something over him (his body? his shirt?), pick him up like a football and run into the house. Once that had been easy — Hank really was a blond then, with tiny fresh limbs, and he would pummel Edward with miniature red tennis shoes while he carried him. Hank's hair was dark brown now, dark as Edward's own had been, and the last time he'd seen him it was two feet long. Edward dropped his arm. Goddamn showoff kid — everything about him was too much.

"You forgot the acne scars."

Hank grinned. "So y'all've met him? America's hope, Hodges, boy dick?"

He didn't trust himself to speak. He flipped through his keys for the one that opened the kitchen door.

"I'd rather not go in," Hank said quickly. "We could go down to the yard if you like." He started down the stairs to the back. "Ella's not home, is she?"

"Since when do you call her Ella?" he called, but Hank pretended not to hear.

Near the bottom of the yard four fruit trees sprawled down the hill, ending in a tangle of blackberry vines along the redwood fence. Hank walked down to the fence, pushed a few vines to one side, then climbed back up to a sloppy apple.

Edward strode straight down to him and took hold of his arms. "What the hell do you think you're doing? What the hell are you mixed up in?"

Hank was not nearly as tall as he was, and he had to bend his neck back to look up at Edward. After a moment, Edward let him go, turned away and snapped some unnecessary twigs off the pear tree. He flung them away, disgusted with himself for doing anything so obvious.

Hank leaned casually back against the trunk of the apple, crossing his arms and pretending total nonchalance. "So. It seems that you and Wonderboy had quite a chat. What did you talk about? If you don't mind my asking."

The afternoon sun reflected bright off the bay into Edward's eyes. He wanted to screen them but instinctively didn't, as if that would weaken his position. He moved so that Hank's body blocked some of the light.

"You tell me."

Hank produced a mild smile. "Oh, I know what he thinks. I'm here to make sure you didn't take him seriously. He likes to think he's after one of the pivotal criminal minds of our time. It makes him feel —"

"Which you're not?"

"Dad." Hank took off his sunglasses, pressed his nose between thumb and index finger, and squinted at the glare — his eyes were like Ella's, pale and tender with a myopic bulge and overly sensitive to light. "Dad. Guys in San Quentin do not talk to punk kid radicals. Oh, sure, we talked big. We were going to overthrow the government, save the world. A major threat to the bourgeois order. There was Alcibiades, there was Batman, and now there's Hank Hooper . . . Do you really think we fooled anyone? Nobody, I mean nobody, takes us seriously except the FBI." He held the sunglasses by their stems and gestured at his body. "Can you blame them? Look at me. I'm strictly Hollywood."

"So why have you gone underground?"

He shrugged. "We couldn't fool *ourselves* otherwise."

Edward kept his voice down. "I saw a photo-graph. A guy in San Quentin was talking to a punk kid radical."

"Ah," Hank said. He looked down and sucked his lower lip, looking very much the way he had at three. His neck was bent in a fragile arc, and sun glared through the bleached stubble on his head. Edward let it hang there for a moment.

"Look," he began, but Hank held up his hand and stared at him fiercely.

"You know, Dad, I would have appreciated this sort of attention when I was five. But it's a little late now."

Edward stepped back.

"I mean, why change your style now? Your who-gives-a-damn style? Your patented let-them-eat-cake approach to parenthood? Oh, don't get me wrong — we never minded it. We were the envy of all our friends. Of course, it was a little disturbing, the way it seemed to have no limits. That's what I was doing half the time, trying to find some. I wanted you to tell me to stop. But you never did."

Edward paced a few steps, wanting to get it right: he knew he didn't have much time. "It wasn't disability — it was policy. You challenged, and I failed to answer. It was practice for life."

Hank seemed to be listening to something in the distance. He took a step down toward the fence. A car door slammed, close by, in the driveway. Heavy feet in hard shoes trod the deck.

"Wait!" Edward lunged for him, but his son was in the blackberry vines, shirt snagging on thorns. Hauling himself up the fence with hands and knees, Hank sprawled across the top and disappeared without a backward glance.

Hodges and the others didn't waste much time — the green car roared out of the driveway after Hank. Minutes later, Edward was dropping downhill on the bike, disguised in a pair of David's threadbare jeans, a gray sweatshirt, the black leather jacket, dark glasses, David's black motorcycle boots and a backwards Yankees cap.

He pushed through the door of the bank minutes before it closed. The only account he could touch without Ella's signature contained less than three hundred dollars, and he took it all in cash.

He found a pay phone and decided what to say — he would only have a moment. The phone rang eighteen times, then stopped. Someone had picked it up without saying hello.

"Hank's father is leaving money for him in the backyard of the house where Hank used to live."

The person on the other end said nothing but did not hang up. He said it again. "Got that?" The phone went dead.

He rode past the brown-shingled house and parked down the block. Sitting on the bike, he watched the street until he was sure he hadn't been followed. He walked by the house, turned back and ducked up the drive.

The backyard was barren and dusty, all dry weeds and thistles. There was no place to leave the money, not even an old chair. He took off the jacket, folded it, and set it in the middle of what had once been the lawn. The money was in the inside pocket.

He walked back to the bike and straddled it. He should drive away — he knew that. Whoever was coming might wait until he was gone, and if it was Hank, he should do it fast or not at all. If Hodges had that number bugged, he might get the message before Hank and be here to meet him.

He turned the bike, but went on watching the house in the rearview mirror. Was that Hank, two blocks away — a blond kid, walking? He should get out of sight, he should be — no. The kid turned in at a different house.

Suddenly he remembered how he'd gotten into that yard a few hours before — you didn't need to come down this street at all. He let go of the bike and ran back to the yard, stumbling slightly in the heeled boots.

The jacket was gone. Leaping the honeysuckle fence, he ran out to the street behind. He could see for blocks in every direction. But there was no one, walking toward him or away from him, anywhere around.

NOW YOU
SEE IT

❖❖❖

ONE FALL MORNING, my father woke up and died. I doubt he knew such a thing could happen to him, or even that it was happening when it did. He was just past fifty and seemed younger than he was, one of those tall boyish men who look the same way most of their lives. He still liked the same kind of shirts he wore at Harvard (button-down oxfords, white with blue stripes), still put the same brand of cherry tobacco in his pipe.

He didn't act twenty-five, however. If you said something to him, he never answered right away. He'd scrape out his pipe and seem to be thinking only about that. Then he'd say something you didn't want to hear. That it was nice of me to wear a skirt that showed the boys how the thigh bone was connected to the hip bone. That, given my boyfriend's verbal skills, he must be the sexual equivalent of a slam dunk.

When he said things like that, you could tell it wasn't funny to him, though he pretended all he cared about was making smart remarks. He loved jokes about the bomb, and after he told one he'd chuckle quietly, heh-heh-heh, watching you, while his eyes got shiny and wet. If he heard that a baby, anyone's baby, was born with an open spine, he went around for days with his face hollowed out, but he could also tell the only funny baby-with-an-open-spine jokes you ever heard.

He couldn't sleep more than a few hours, and usually he stayed up reading and writing until dawn. His last night on earth, he left the table before dessert, and the light in his study was still on when my mother and I went to sleep. Sweet smoke drifted under his door, fanned up the stairs, glided under our beds.

In the early morning, he took a nap on the leather couch in his study and woke up feeling sick to his stomach. He told my mother, then went to their bedroom and lay down on top of the covers. When she went in an hour later to see how he was, he was dead.

◈◈◈

My mother decided not to call the high school, since there was nothing anyone could do. As usual I took the bus up Euclid, got off at our street and climbed the steep hill, past the neighbors' pink camellias, red bottlebrush, white oleander, tall bushes all studded with blooms. I held my bookbag loosely in one hand, letting it rub along the sidewalk.

I hated to go home with nothing to do. When my brothers were kids, I could count on war games in the yard, basketball in the driveway. One of them might be in the garden experimenting with bugs (can a beetle keep going with five legs? two legs? one?) or just in the mood to chase me down and tickle me till my eyes popped out. When they got older, they blasted radios on different stations, slammed doors, gunned motorcycles, hit tennis balls against the house, even shouted in their sleep. One night I woke up and heard two of them going at once. "Hey, hey, hey," Hank yelled in the room next to mine, then "Cut it!" someone shouted down the hall, David or Charlie, I couldn't tell which.

Now the whole house was quiet. As I got closer, I could hear it absorbing sound, like a black hole. It was a square brown house, set down the hill from the road, surrounded by dark green cedars.

My oldest brother's car was in the driveway. It was a black Porsche with a shelf sticking out of its rearend like a giant stinger, to keep the back tires on the road at speeds much faster than he was likely to go. I stood looking at it for a minute. Charlie was not my favorite brother. Probably he couldn't help the way he was — with two brothers close behind him, he couldn't afford to be generous to anyone. But I had almost no good memories connected with him. He could hold my wrists like handcuffs or dangle me upside down by the ankles for an hour. He was the only one who never asked my advice about a girl, and the only one who thought he had to find out every detail about my private life.

I stepped quietly down the stairs to the deck. If Charlie was there, it meant that something had happened, or was going to happen. He was an engineer now, working for an oil company and out of the country half the time. When he did come over he got in terrible fights with our father. Charlie hated what was going on at Berkeley, and since Dad taught there and had what Charlie considered anti-American views, he held Dad personally responsible. It was especially bad now that Hank had gone to Cuba. He went there with some other students to pick sugar cane and get the Cuban economy off the ground, and Charlie said that meant he was a man without a country and ought to be shot. My other brother, David, was in Vietnam, but he was a more tolerant kind of person and said everyone had to do what they believed was right.

I edged up to the glass door into the kitchen and looked in. My mother was talking on the wall phone

166

and Charlie was braced against the refrigerator, his body rigid, red eyes fixed unblinking on the ceiling as if he expected to be yanked out of the room and launched into space.

I decided I wasn't in any hurry to find out what was going on in there. I left my bookbag on the deck and went down into the garden. It was October, but the sun was warm and full, as if night and winter had been called off forever. We were high up the hill overlooking the bay, and from the yard you could see San Francisco, three major bridges and the coastal mountains. The water was a different color every day, gray or green, cobalt on cold sunny days, brown after a heavy rain. Today it was a lighthearted blue.

At the bottom of the garden was a row of ghost gums, white eucalyptus so thin they bent in the wind like wheat. We had a rope swing hanging from the lowest branch of one, and I went down to look at it, standing on the pointy, menthol-smelling nuts in my light sandals. The rope was fat and mushy from being left out through about twelve rainy seasons, and I didn't think it would hold me anymore. I pulled down on it and it groaned, relaxed and lengthened under my hands, as if it were about to pull apart.

I climbed up to the middle terrace and lay down on the grass, face up to the sun. Looking through the pink veil of my eyelids, I couldn't feel my body, only the hot yellow sun. If I opened my eyes a crack, I could see bloodcells zooming around in a network of capillaries, like tiny cars on a freeway cloverleaf.

I heard the kitchen door slide open and the deck creak. The grass was dry from the long season of no rain, and it crackled under the footsteps. They were easy and light, not like my brother's. Charlie was big, quick and dangerous. If he wanted to sneak up on you, he definitely could.

I ran over what I had done lately. The day before, I had cut two classes for important personal reasons, but the counselor did not call me in, so I figured they were tired of prosecuting me. Maybe my mother had found out about the far worse things I had done all summer, here on this lawn and sometimes in my own room. Maybe Charlie had come over to tell her. I sat up and squinted at her, waiting to see what it was.

❖❖❖

My mother grew up in Germany and Switzerland, and at fifty she still looked like a girl mountaineer. She had a strong jaw, a dark tan and alpine hair coiled on top of her head. The only lines in her face were the furrows leading to her muscular lips, tensed always with the perfect pronunciations of German, English, Italian, French.

She tried sometimes to teach us German, and if we made a mistake she corrected us, a little triumphantly, before we finished the sentence. She was once a champion swimmer, and she coached us, one knee on the deck, arms cocked at the perfect angle, stroking through the air, turning her chin just enough to get a breath above the imaginary water, while we stood shivering, watching her, in the real water below. She taught us to do things California children never did, such as stand when an adult came into the room, say "ma'am" and "sir," and "lie" instead of "lay."

She was an amateur photographer, good enough to sell a few pictures, and she spent most of her time walking around Berkeley looking for something to shoot. When she was home, she worked in the darkroom in the basement or helped my father with his research, looking up page numbers for footnotes and typing his articles on her old manual. While she was typing, if she came to something she didn't like, she changed it.

"What have you done here, Ella?" I remember him saying, coming into the kitchen, pointing to a passage with his pipe stem.

She glanced at it without bending her neck, as if it wasn't worth the trouble, and lifted a hand to her hair to see if it was coming down. Fingering the mass on top, she pushed the pins in, one by one.

"Could that be where you said that factories have 'an odor of tragedy'?"

"Yes, that was it. And your objection?"

In spite of herself, she started to grin. "Doesn't that sound to you a little bit, how shall I say — romantic?"

He put the pipe carefully between his lips and retired to his study. Hours later he came out, strode down to the darkroom and said something that was probably clever and biting. On his way back up he took the stairs two at a time, looking ruffled but alert. A moment later she breezed up, opened the study door and said something in her deep voice, laughing. She brushed down the stairs, grinning as if she had just taken his queen.

She didn't take many pictures while my brothers were growing up. Taller than she was by the age of twelve, they gathered around her, demanding French toast, creased pants, justice for the wrongs they did each other. She was constantly in motion, like a canary trying to raise hawks.

"Watch this pot, Jane," she would say, handing me a wooden spoon. Or "Get that, would you?" when the phone rang while she was tying a tie, slipping an egg on a plate. If I was going downtown, would I pick up some basil, a baguette, a roll of Kodak Tri-X?

The first summer after the boys had all left home, I went out on the deck early one morning and heard her below me in the garden. She was singing in a low voice. Every few words she hit a high note hard and paused.

"The girls in — white dresses — are going — to town —"

I slid up to the railing in my bare feet and looked over.

Facing out toward the bay, hands on hips in gardening gloves, she was doing high kicks. She arched her back, hopped and threw one leg up straight, foot as high as her head. She sang the same line over and over.

"The girls in — white dresses — are going — to town —"

Her most famous photograph was of me, when I was a year old. It was Christmas Eve, my first on my feet, and we had real candles on the tree, German-style. She set the camera up on a tripod half inside the branches to get a closeup of my reaction. I staggered up to the glowing tree and reached out experimentally. In the picture the candle is in the foreground, my chubby finger in the fire. She caught the candlelight reflected in my eyes and my half-smile about to open on a shriek.

❖❖❖

She wore gray at the funeral, since she considered black a foolish and romantic color. My American grandmother flew out from New York, and for her sake my mother had the service in an Episcopal church, though my father never went near a church of any kind. There was no coffin. She had him cremated the day after he died, and she did not let us see the body.

We had not been able to reach Hank in Cuba, but David flew two days to get here, had one day at home, and flew two days back. He was a medic in Vietnam, and when he found out there was no body to see, he stood around with his hands hanging out of his uniform sleeves, glaring out the windows. The rest of us sat at the kitchen table. Once when my mother was out of the room he turned away from the window.

"How did this happen, Charlie? He was way too young. Didn't any of you guys know he was sick?"

Charlie got up, staring at David with his lips ajar. He took a step toward him, stopped, dropped his arms. "Gee, David. That's a good point. Maybe it wouldn't have happened if you'd been around. Maybe you could have laid your hands on him." He turned and strode out of the room.

David flicked a glance over me as he turned back to the window, the way he might have looked at a cat or a chair. He bunched his fist around the cord for the window shade. I could see one side of his face reflected in the glass, against a cedar outside. His mouth opened, lips pulled back taut toward his ear. His shoulders vibrated but he didn't make a sound. A moment later he smoothed out his face, let go of the cord and stood looking out the window.

Our grandmother wanted to take the ashes back with her to put in the cemetery with her family, but my mother said no. David was gone by that time, Charlie had to fly to Japan, and my grandmother must have assumed my mother was going to put the ashes in a graveyard in Berkeley. Nobody else asked what she planned to do with them.

The day after my grandmother flew home, my mother let me miss another day of school. We drove to a cemetery in the Oakland hills, stopped at a building near the entrance and picked up the ashes.

The box was white, bigger than I expected and weighed more than it ought to for its size. I got my arms around it and at first it seemed heavy but manageable. Halfway to the car it almost slid out of my hands. It pulled hard toward the ground, like anti-matter or a piece of an imploded star. My mother went ahead to open the door, and I ran with it the last few feet. On the way home she drove and it sat on my lap, pressing into my thighs, digging in its edges on the turns.

She didn't say anything, and I didn't ask where

we were going. She drove to Berkeley, up to the top of the ridge, turned up our street and dropped down the steep drive. She set the brake, got out and came around to my side.

The wind blew wisps of fine hair across her face. She stood by the car, gathered them up, gave them a twist and pushed them under a pin. Her face was grim like a piece of rock, but right away the breeze set free another halo of jolly wisps, frolicking around it.

She slid her strong fingers between me and the box. "Tip it this way while you get out."

We held it on our bent hands, facing each other.

"Carefully now. We will go in the front door."

We stepped sideways along the flagstone path. She rested her side on the edge of a planter while she opened the door. One stair at a time, we went up three flights to the attic.

The roof was low and we had to stoop to get under the beams. She picked a spot well back from the eaves. We crouched slowly, easing it down, but it picked up speed, slid out of our hands and slammed onto the pine planks, poofing up a swirl of dust.

She moved it a little this way, a little that. She straightened it so the corners were square with the attic.

"That's all right." She stood up and looked around. She gathered up the stray hairs, then let them go. "Look at all this mess. We should throw some of it out."

We carried down boxes of my brothers' toys, comic books and other treasures they had made her keep and then forgotten. I found two cartons of my father's papers — minutes from meetings of the tenure committee, notes and handouts from decades of classes. Some of them had his doodles in the margins. He had made it an art, elaborate abstract designs in three or four colors. Sometimes he drew something ordinary, a train or a Christmas tree or a boat, then filled it in with red sunbursts, yellow slashes, blue globes. We had hundreds of his doodles. His desk was full of them, and through the years he had mounted the best to hang on the tree at Christmas. When we were kids he used to put them on our lunchbags, and I found one once on a box of snail pellets in the garage.

I showed the papers to my mother. She glanced through them as she dropped them by the handfuls in the trash.

⬧⬧⬧

Sometimes that winter, when she was out shooting, I went up to the attic. I needed to convince myself that he was dead. I was used to people going away, being there one day and gone the next, and I half expected him to start writing home, like David and Hank. Hank's last letter had arrived two months after Daddy died. *Viva la revolución,* it said at the end. He never got the telegrams we sent, and he thought he was writing to his father.

At one end of the attic, a window let in gray light. Fresh cold air leaked in around the trapdoor to the roof, low down on one side near the eaves. I lay down on the dusty planks and wrapped my body around the box.

I remembered things about him. When he passed my mother's list (eggs, Lysol, milk) posted on the refrigerator, he added items to it (frankincense, wolfsbane, eye of newt). When he shot baskets with my brothers in front of the garage, he played hard, got red in the face, but if Charlie started to care too much, he'd lob it over his head and bounce-pass between his legs. Once Charlie arrived at the dinner table and announced that David could not come down because he was in his room practicing solitary vice. Daddy looked at the ceiling.

"Solitary vice, let's see — that's eating cookie dough?"

I told myself that all of that was in the box. I wrapped tighter around it, holding it with my knees and arms. Every so often a floorboard snapped.

As the winter went on and rain rumbled on the

attic roof, I started to wonder why she brought it home. I never saw her go up there, and she didn't even seem to think about it. I thought about it all the time. Whatever I was doing in the house I could feel it up there, white and heavy over my head. Why didn't she notice it?

I started to wonder about other things. Didn't she know the Seven Warning Signals of Heart Attacks? Why didn't she go in sooner to see how he was? She could have tried a little CPR. And when was the last time he had a checkup? I almost felt like, if she gave me a straight answer about things like that, she could have a second chance and do it right.

I spent whole afternoons leaning against the box, seething. We became a sort of club against my mother.

Downstairs, her life went on pretty much as usual. She had never had close friends, and she seemed happy to work alone all day, make supper for me and spend the evening reading. She read journals about photography and science, and lately she had started reading books about physics.

I was doing even worse than usually in school and she had made me sign up for physics on the theory that I'd get excited about that — she had done it herself once, a couple of light-years ago, when she was in college. One night I sat at the dining room table, pretending to do time-and-distance calculations. She hovered over me, flipping through the pages of my textbook.

"Hurry up and finish this part, it is too elementary. This is not the important stuff here. Get to the particles, that's what you want to know about."

She seemed so happy, so exuberant, talking about physics that I started to hate the whole subject. How could she care about such a thing, when Daddy was dead?

"Look at this." She picked up my clear plastic pen. "Forget what it looks like. The truth is, it is not a stable solid thing, the way it looks. The truth is, it's a wild dance of particles too small to see. And the strange thing is, it's not that the particles are *doing* a dance — they *are* the dance." She grinned with her strong lips, watching me. "Do you see? Yes? Matter and energy are the same thing. Forget what the book says — that is what they have discovered at the subatomic level. The smallest particles they know about aren't little pieces of dirt spinning around — if you take away the spinning, *there is no dirt*. Do you see what that means? No?" She held my pen up and zoomed it around in the air. "It means that everything is dancing. Everything is flying — matter, everything. Matter is dancing. Maybe a better way to say it might be —" She laughed, lifted a hand to her hair. "Every flying is thing?"

I looked at her morosely, and she put down the pen. She shrugged. "But I guess you do not care about that. Too bad." She went back to the living room and her book.

❖•❖•❖

One Saturday morning, when I went up to the attic, the box was open. I stood looking at it, afraid to get closer. I reached out a bare foot and nudged up one of the flaps. It was completely empty.

Then I noticed, nearby on the floor, a sort of covered pot, made of white marble. Its lid was off, and there was nothing in it. I got down on my knees and ran a finger around the curved interior, smooth and cool and clean.

I felt a burst of cool air and looked up. The trapdoor to the roof was open. Crouching under the low roof, I approached it cautiously. I couldn't hear anything unusual, so I peeked out, over the sill, squinting in the bright sun.

There was nobody out there. The trapdoor led to the uphill side of the roof, overlooking the street — it was three stories to the ground and we were not allowed to go out there. Sometimes I climbed over the peak of the roof to the downhill side, which you couldn't see from anywhere, to hide out and sunbathe. Nobody ever figured out where I was.

I pulled my head back into the attic and looked at the boxes again. I was getting mad. What right did she have to do that? What did she care?

I started at the top of the house and worked my way down. I don't know what I was looking for, but I checked every room and every closet. I got all the way down to the basement without finding anything.

No one was allowed to go into the darkroom, and I knew I was trespassing when I opened the door. The cold air smelled of chemicals and the cement was icy under my feet. For a minute I couldn't find the string for the light. Inching my hand through the dark, I felt it slip over my fingers. I grabbed it and the hard light came on.

She didn't have a closet. I checked her drawers and looked around the jugs of chemicals and stacks of printing paper on the floor.

The first photographs I noticed were in the trash, about fifty of them, dropped in one stack into a big garbage can. They were portraits of my Dad's study. His empty chair, pulled out as if he had just left it, his pipe on the desk. The chair pushed in and everything lined up as if no one had ever worked there. Pictures of his books on the shelves, standing up straight, falling over, spilling out onto the floor. She liked the action shot best, books in motion, tumbling end over end, cracked open, pages fluttering. There were about twenty of those.

On her workbench was another series, of gravestones. They had blurred edges, comet trails of light, as if they were moving at high speed. The latest ones, up on the drying rack, seemed to be pictures of light. Light springing off a polished stone, bounding up an obelisk, glancing off a puddle and spearing you in the eye.

I pulled out her chair and started to sit down, but I noticed something was on it. It was her photo bag. David had made it for her years ago, when he was trying to make a living selling purses on Telegraph Avenue. It was handstitched out of a single piece of leather, on a design she had given him herself, and she never went anywhere without it.

The hair stood up on the back of my neck as I backed out of the room. I found the basement door, opened it, walked out fast into the bright garden.

It was one of those weeks of sudden spring we get toward the end of winter, cold grass and the sky so blue it hurts, but the sun warm enough to lie out naked. Crocuses, daffodils and tulips had all sprung up, and hummingbirds were fighting over them.

One hovered by a red tulip, and while I watched another zoomed in. With a roar of wings, they charged each other and took off tumbling and cheeping at high speed. Passing over me, their heads gleamed red, then green, then red. The winner came back and landed on a twig, shrinking from winged glory to miniature brown bird.

I looked all over the garden and did not find her. I felt tired and sad. I went up to the deck, lay down on a bench and closed my eyes.

I don't know how long I lay there, or if I really fell asleep. I could smell warm redwood under me, but my body felt weightless, and I seemed to be drifting through a gold mist. Soon I was back in the attic. The roof was gone and light shone upward from the floor to the sky. My mother was there, and in front of us was the box. As we watched, its white shell cracked, broke slowly open, and my father hatched out. He had a skeptical, intelligent look on his face and huge white wings. They were cramped by the tight space but, rustling, gleaming yellow and blue and pink, feather by feather they unfolded. He flapped them once or twice, put his pipe in his mouth and took hold of my mother's hand. They took off and kept rising until they disappeared from sight.

I sat up blinking. I went to the glass door of the

kitchen, slid it open and went in. On the table, propped against a glass of milk, was a note.

Jane,
  I am on the roof. Please come up when you've had your breakfast.

I picked it up and ran to the attic. Climbing out the trapdoor, I scaled the warm green shingles. The soles of my feet were a little too smooth, but I had learned long ago that if I kept moving forward I would not slip. I crested the peak, put one leg over it for balance, and I could see the downhill side.

She was sitting near the edge, and it was four stories to the ground on this side. I sat afraid to move, afraid to scare her — was she going to jump? She had her arms around a brown grocery sack with the top rolled down — that would be the ashes. Was she going to jump, clutching them? Her camera was strapped to her back, and she appeared to be looking peacefully out over the bay.

I slid down to her, slowly and carefully.

"Mom," I said. "Mom."

She turned to me and smiled. "Is it not a perfect morning? No wind."

She held the bag out toward me, but I only looked at it.

"Take that, please," she said. "Now, stand here.

Can you? Brace yourself against the chimney. That's right. Now wait till I tell you to start."

She climbed back up the peak and straddled it, gripping the shingles with the knees of her khaki pants.

"Start what?"

The black camera hid her face, pointing at me. She contorted on the peak, trying for angles.

"I want you to throw them. Just a few at a time. Make them last. Take a handful and throw it up. Right up over your head, as high as you can. Do you understand? Wait until I say to start. All right. Good. Now. Go ahead now."

Slowly I unrolled the bag and looked inside. Something gray puffed up into the sun. I thought they would be heavy and gritty, maybe even sticky or greasy, clump in my hand and patter on the roof, but when I slid my hand in the bag, they were dry, and fine, and light as baby powder. It was impossible to give them any direction. No matter which way I threw them or how hard, they made a swarm like gnats and faded into blue sky or blue water.

The camera clicked and whirred.

"Not over there — this way more — the background's wrong there. That is better. Can you get them higher?"

I threw some low, trying to see them pepper the

roof, but they were gone before they got there. I threw them straight up over my head, and they vanished, like a shout in the air. The bag was empty before I knew it.

"Stay away from that side — please, I told you. Keep them high. Why are you stopping?"

I held the bag open and shook. Pale smoke drifted out like spores from a puffball.

"Why are you stopping? Do not stop! Throw some now!"

I opened the bag wide and turned it this way and that, trying to catch a breeze. I flattened it out and shook it.

"Go ahead! Throw some now!"

I folded the bag.

She yanked the camera away from her face. "What are you doing? It is never empty. You threw them too fast!"

She examined the camera, holding it out at arm's length so she could read the dial. "Shake the bag out. There must be some more."

I unfolded it for her and waved it around. Nothing came out. I refolded it and climbed up beside her.

She was putting the camera back in its case. "I wish you had listened to me about that. I wish you hadn't thrown them so fast. I hardly got anything."

"Maybe you got all there was."

She tightened the camera strap across her chest, pressing her lips together.

She eyed the steep slope down. "How does one do this? You have been up here before."

"Did you know that?" I grinned at her, but she didn't notice. "Like this," I said. "Don't look down."